'I really, ⋯⋯⋯⋯⋯⋯⋯⋯⋯
hospital n⋯⋯⋯⋯⋯⋯⋯⋯
me banan⋯⋯⋯⋯⋯⋯⋯⋯
gritted te⋯⋯⋯⋯⋯⋯⋯⋯
you were planning on being our
locum for a while… Have you got
digs lined up?'

Uh-oh. She had a nasty feeling she knew what
was coming. 'I'm staying at The Limes.'

'I've got a better solution,' Will said. 'My spare
room. If you stay at the cottage there'll be a
doctor on the premises if I get into trouble, so
they'll let me out.'

Yeah, right.

He grimaced. 'Mallory, this wasn't—isn't—an
attempt to seduce you. Sharing my cottage until
I'm fit again doesn't mean I'm expecting you to
share my bed or anything like that.'

Her skin heated again. She hadn't been thinking
along those lines at all. Although now he'd
mentioned it… No. He might be drop-dead
gorgeous, beneath the bruising and the plaster,
but she *wasn't* going to have an affair with Will
Cooper. She was going to be sensible, and make
sure her working partnerships stayed work only.
'I didn't think you were.'

Kate Hardy lives on the outskirts of Norwich with her husband, two small children, two lazy spaniels—and too many books to count! She wrote her first book at six, when her parents gave her a typewriter for her birthday. She had the first of a series of sexy romances published at twenty-five, and swapped a job in marketing communications for freelance health journalism when her son was born so she could spend more time with him. She's wanted to write for Mills & Boon® since she was twelve—and when she was pregnant with her daughter her husband pointed out that writing Medical Romances™ would be the perfect way to combine her interest in health issues with her love of good stories. It really is the best of both worlds—especially as she gets to meet a new gorgeous hero every time...

Recent titles by the same author:

A BABY OF HER OWN
HIS EMERGENCY FIANCÉE
HER SPECIAL CHILD
THE ITALIAN DOCTOR'S PROPOSAL

THE DOCTOR'S RESCUE

BY
KATE HARDY

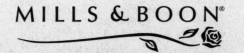

MILLS & BOON

For my father, John Roy Sewell, with love

All the characters in this book have no existence outside the imagination of the author, and have no relation whatsoever to anyone bearing the same name or names. They are not even distantly inspired by any individual known or unknown to the author, and all the incidents are pure invention.

First published in Great Britain 2004
Harlequin Mills & Boon Limited,
Eton House, 18-24 Paradise Road, Richmond, Surrey TW9 1SR

© Pamela Brooks 2004

ISBN 0 263 83875 7

Set in Times Roman 10½ on 11½ pt.
03-0104-50294

Printed and bound in Spain
by Litografia Rosés, S.A., Barcelona

CHAPTER ONE

'Go 'WAY, Gnome,' Will slurred. 'Wan' sleep.'

'No, you don't, sunshine. You're really, really not going to sleep now. Stay awake for me.'

Bright blue eyes stared at him from under the even brighter yellow hood. Not fair, torturing him like this. His leg hurt, his head hurt, his arm hurt, and all he wanted to do was go to sleep. But the gnome was shining a light in his eyes and wouldn't let him.

'What's your name?' Her voice was gentler this time. Like her hands, which stroked his face tenderly. Lovely hands.

'It's W—'

Then everything faded, and he sank into sweet oblivion.

Everything hurt. Absolutely everything. Will risked moving an eyelid and closed it again quickly. The light was too bright. But he couldn't go back to sleep again now—there was too much noise. People talking, clattering sounds and beeping. Sounds that were familiar somehow and yet strange at the same time. Where was he?

Resignedly, he opened his eyes. And saw her sitting cross-legged in the chair at the foot of his bed, reading a book. The gnome. Not a gnome—an elf, he decided, now she wasn't wearing that huge yellow waterproof.

She smiled and put the book down. 'Well, I suppose an elf's an improvement on a gnome.'

Oh, no. He couldn't have actually *said* that.

''Fraid so.'

'Wha—?'

She uncrossed her legs, stood up and came over to the bed. 'Would you like some water?'

He nodded gratefully. She wasn't an elf either, then. More like an angel.

If angels had spiky auburn hair. Weren't they supposed to be all golden and shining? And he couldn't see any sign of wings or a halo.

Though she didn't make a comment, so he clearly hadn't spoken aloud this time.

She held a plastic beaker and put the straw to his lips, and he took a sip. And another. And another. And then she took the beaker away.

'Not too much at once,' she said.

Will resented that, even though her tone was kind. Didn't she know his mouth felt as if it had been stuffed with sawdust? He needed water. *Lots* more water. He glowered at her and started to reach over to where she'd put the beaker on the bedside cabinet. Then he realised he had no chance of getting the water. Because his left arm was encased in plaster.

He stared at it in disbelief. He had a broken arm?

Her quiet voice cut into his thoughts. 'Can you remember what happened?'

Will's eyes widened. Oh, yes, he remembered what happened. The car coming round the corner in Darrowthwaite high street, the look of horror on the driver's face when he saw the little girl run into the road and realised he wouldn't be able to stop in time, the screech of tyres and the smell of burning rubber as he'd slammed on the brakes…

And then the impact. The bone-jarring impact when the car had thudded into him.

'Car,' he forced out.

'Anything else?'

He looked suspiciously at her. 'Are you a reporter?'

'No.' She changed tack again. 'Do you know what day it is?'

'Thursday.' He suddenly realised why she was asking. She wanted to check if he had amnesia. 'How long was I out?'

'The second time, you mean?'

So he'd been knocked out *twice*?

'Only for about fifteen minutes.' She gave him a rueful smile. 'You gave us all a scare.'

'I'm fine now. I'm going...' His voice faded as he tried to sit up. No, he wasn't going to swing his legs over the side of the bed. He had a nasty feeling he knew exactly why his right leg had a dressing taped over it: the car had given him more than just a bruise. A *lot* more.

He stared at her. 'Who are you?'

'My name's Mallory Ryman.'

It didn't ring any bells. And Mallory Ryman was definitely a woman once seen, never forgotten. Small and slender, with huge blue eyes and a mouth that...

Stop right there, Will Cooper. You're in hospital with an arm in plaster and probably a pinned leg, you ache all over, you've probably got concussion and you're in no fit condition to start thinking like that about her, he told himself.

And then he panicked. Was it more than just concussion making him feel groggy? *Did* he know Mallory? Did she work with him? Was she a neighbour? Or was *she* the one who'd managed to melt his resolve about never getting involved again?

'Can you remember your name?'

Uh-oh. This was beginning to sound as if he *did* know her. So why couldn't he remember who she was? 'I'm Will Cooper.'

She smiled. 'Good. That's what your notes say, too. And what I was told in Darrowthwaite.'

He relaxed again. It was all right. He didn't have amnesia

on top of everything else. Though a tiny part of him was disappointed. As if he'd been hoping that she—

No. He'd already learned the hard way that love didn't exist.

'I thought you might like an update on the little girl.'

'Little girl?' Will parroted.

'The reason you're in here,' Mallory told him kindly.

As if he'd forgotten. His mind was just working a bit more slowly than usual, that was all. 'Kelly Beswick. Is she all right?'

'Not so much as a bruise on her. You took all the impact and your body cushioned hers,' Mallory said. 'Her mum was in shock, mind. I had to prescribe some hot sweet tea.'

So his gnome—elf—angel—whatever—had a sense of humour. Because, of course, Will, being a GP in Darrowthwaite, should have been the one doing the prescribing. No doubt Wendy Beswick had told Mallory who he was.

'But Kelly's fine. The driver had a bit of a sore neck so they're checking him out in Casualty—it's probably minor whiplash. And Wendy's going to keep Kelly on reins in future, particularly the next time she starts chatting to her friends in the middle of the street. I think she's realised now that two-year-olds have a low boredom threshold. Especially when they see a cat on the other side of the road—'

'And step straight out in front of a car,' Will finished.

'Lucky you saw it and got her out of the way.'

Mallory didn't need to elaborate. They both knew that the impact would have killed the small child. Will had seen the toddler wander into the road, then the car come round the corner. There was only one thing he could possibly have done—and he'd done it. Rushed into the road, even though it had felt like wading through treacle at the time, and scooped her out of the way, taking the brunt of the impact himself.

The dull thud had reverberated through his body. And then he'd hit the tarmac.

'And even luckier it wasn't summer,' Mallory said.

He knew exactly what she meant. In summer, he wouldn't have been wearing a waxed thornproof jacket. He'd have been in shirtsleeves—thin fabric that would have been torn to shreds on the tarmac when he'd hit it. And as for the skin underneath… It didn't bear thinking about.

'Anyway, I told Wendy I'd come to the hospital and let you know that the little girl was all right.'

'Thanks.' She hadn't needed to do that. And he appreciated it. He gave her a half-smile, then the aches in his body made him wince again. 'Sorry I wrecked your holiday.'

'Holiday?' she tested.

OK, so the first week of January wasn't the most popular time of year for a holiday in the Lakes. But she was definitely on holiday. It was obvious, wasn't it? He gestured with his free hand. 'Proper walking boots. Bright yellow waterproof.' She wasn't wearing it but he could see it draped over the back of her chair. His gaze dropped to the floor next to the chair. 'Rucksack.' And, since her boots looked well worn and he recognised them as an expensive make, she was clearly a seasoned walker—a climber even, though she looked too slender and fragile to have the strength for rock-climbing.

Please, don't let her be a climber.

'Nice deduction, Mr Holmes,' she teased. 'Though actually, I'm not on holiday as such.' Her smile faded. 'And, if anything, I owe *you*.'

'How come?'

She shook her head. 'It's not important. Anyway, you should be resting.'

'I *am* resting,' he pointed out wryly. He couldn't move from his bed. Not without crutches, anyway, if his leg was pinned. And a quick glance around his cubicle showed no sign of crutches. So he was definitely stuck here. Great. He had a million and one things to do, clinics to run and lists to work through and paperwork to finish off and…

He must have spoken aloud again because she nodded. 'And you feel as if you've been run over by a steamroller.'

'Yeah,' he admitted.

Mallory checked his chart. 'You're due some analgesics. I'll go and tell the nurse you're ready for them.'

She'd said 'analgesics', not 'painkillers', Will noted. And then he remembered the way she'd checked his pupils moments after the accident. Probably after he'd blacked out—that was why she'd checked his pupils in the first place. 'You're a doctor,' he said.

'Was,' she said grimly, and left the cubicle.

Was? What did she mean, *was*? Had she been struck off? Or…? His mind refused to make any connections, and he sank back against his pillows. All he could think about right now was the dull ache that beat through his body.

She returned a couple of minutes later with a nurse who carried two white tablets in a small cup.

'Paracetamol?' Will asked hopefully.

Mallory smiled. 'Don't you think you might need just a little bit more than that?'

'Yeah,' he admitted, as another wave of pain shot through him.

'I'll do your obs first,' the nurse said. She checked his temperature, pulse and respiration. Though her hands weren't like Mallory's. They were just as cool and professional, but the touch of her skin hadn't heated his blood the way Mallory's had.

No. Absolutely not. He wasn't going to start thinking of Mallory in those terms.

He sneaked a glance at her. And wished he hadn't when his gaze met hers. It felt as if lightning had just coursed through him. His pulse was racing, too. Not good. How could he explain to the nurse that it wasn't anything to do with the accident? It was…the look of a stranger. A perfect stranger. All he knew about her was her name, her previous occupation and the fact she was here on holiday.

So how on earth could she make him feel like an overgrown, gawky teenager, just with one look? And how on earth could the nurse write so calmly on her chart as if an earthquake hadn't just happened before her eyes—wasn't *still* happening?

'Shall I get him some water to go with the analgesics?' Mallory asked.

'Thanks.' The nurse smiled at her. 'I'll leave him in your capable hands, Dr Ryman.'

'Have you had co-proxamol before?' Mallory asked as the nurse left the cubicle.

'Yes.'

'Any reaction to it at all? Any dizziness, blurred vision, slurring your words?'

'No.' She knew he hurt. Why didn't she just give him the painkillers? 'Are you the ward doctor?' he asked.

'No.' She flushed spectacularly, her face clashing wildly with her hair. And then she went white. Absolutely white.

Will could have kicked himself. Considering that she'd come to his rescue after the accident and now she was looking after him—something she really didn't have to do—he'd been ungracious. Worse, he must have touched some sort of sore nerve. She'd only just told him that she used to be a doctor and, whatever the reason for her not being one now, the pain was clearly still raw. 'Sorry. Didn't mean to be nasty.'

'You're in pain and I'm holding up your pain relief. And I'm sure the ward doctor checked your records before he wrote you up for co-proxamol,' Mallory said. She handed him the cup and waited until he'd tipped the tablets into his mouth before giving him the beaker of water.

'Thanks,' he said when he'd swallowed the tablets.

'Is there anything else you need?' she asked.

A new head, he thought. One that didn't hurt. 'No. I'm fine, thanks,' he said.

'I'll be off, then.'

'Stay a bit longer. Please?' The words were out before he'd even finished thinking them.

'I… Look, you ought to rest.'

At least she was saying no in a nice way. She was probably with someone on her walking trip. He'd already taken up too much of her time. This not-wanting-to-let-her-go type of feeling… Well, the accident must have addled his brains as well as smashed his bones. 'Sorry. Selfish,' he mumbled. 'Your friends…' Must be waiting for her, though he couldn't get the words out.

She shook her head. 'I'm on my own.'

So she *could* stay, if she wanted to. But he'd already wrecked her holiday. 'Too dark to walk now. Sorry.'

'Climb,' she corrected.

Climb. The word slammed into his mind and he flinched. Today had been tough. But it had just become a whole heap worse, raking up old wounds. Climbing had already cost him Roland and Julie—his brother and his fiancée. He really should have moved when it had all happened. Gone somewhere flat and quiet and as far from mountains as he could possibly find.

'Are you all right?' she asked. 'Does something new hurt?'

Only my heart. And that was a long, long time ago, he thought. When my fiancée fell in love with my brother. And I wasn't there when the mountain rescue team needed me. And Roly…

'No. I'm fine.' With an effort, Will pulled his concentration back from the memories of that terrible night. 'I hope the duty doctors are as on the ball as you are.'

'If they are, you'd be better off somewhere else,' she muttered.

He could see the pain in her eyes. The kind of pain he knew only too well, the kind of pain that all the medicine in the world couldn't heal. Because the only way to heal it was to face your demons head on. 'Are you all right?'

'Asks the man with a comminuted fracture of the upper tibia, a fractured radius and concussion,' she quipped. The car crash had shattered the bone in Will's leg, and when the impact had knocked him to the ground, he'd landed on his arm and the bone had snapped.

'Comminuted fracture?'

'Uh-huh. You got off lightly—*just* the tibia and not the fibula as well. And it was a closed fracture.'

She wasn't teasing him. If your tibia broke, the force of the impact normally went through your interosseous membrane, the connective tissue lying between the two lower leg bones, and fractured your fibula as well. The layers of skin and tissues over the area were very thin, which usually meant that the broken bone pierced your skin, known as an 'open fracture'. In Will's case, the bone hadn't gone through the skin.

But a comminuted fracture, meaning that the bone had shattered... There could be only one reason why he didn't have a cast on. 'Internal fixation?' he asked.

Mallory nodded. 'Absolutely. So no weight on that leg until the bone knits together again.'

He closed his eyes. 'Three months.' He'd be stuck, unable to do anything, for three whole months. At least.

'Could be worse,' she said, as if she'd read his mind—though his feelings had probably been written all over his face. 'If it'd been your femur, you'd be in traction so you couldn't even get around on crutches.' If you'd broken your thigh bone, you needed traction to stop the large thigh muscles contracting and interfering with the blood supply, or even displacing the broken bone again. 'And you'd have lost a lot more blood.' Enough even to go into shock.

And she was changing the subject. 'Lucky me,' he said dryly, opening his eyes again. 'But what about you?'

She shrugged. 'I'm fine.'

She didn't look it. Again, the words were out of his mouth before his brain had registered them. His brain definitely wasn't involved because he sounded far more coherent than he felt. 'Why don't you grab a cup of coffee, sit down and tell me about it?'

'Nothing to tell.'

'Looks to me,' he said quietly, 'as if you need someone to listen. I'm not going anywhere. And I'm a doctor—what you tell me is just between us.'

'You need to rest.'

He nodded. 'And I also need something to take my mind off things till the co-proxamol kicks in properly. So talk to me. Tell me what's wrong.'

Will's eyes were what won the argument for him. Serious, yet with a certain warmth and honesty. Eyes that she could trust. Sexy, too…

No! She wasn't going to start thinking that way about him. Even though he was cute. More than cute. Even lying in a hospital bed, in plaster and covered in bruises. Will Cooper was what Renee, her American sister-in-law, would call serious eye-candy. Dark hair that flopped over his forehead, eyes as blue as the sky at the top of a mountain, slight stubble that gave him a piratical look and the suggestion of a dimple in his cheek that would win any argument for him when he smiled.

It would be so easy to give in to the attraction. But

Mallory couldn't. She had nothing to give anyone right now. Not after Geoff. Her eye flicked automatically to Will's left hand. No wedding ring visible, though that didn't prove anything. He was probably married, or at least living with someone. So the chances were he wasn't available anyway.

But she did need to talk. Will was right about that. 'OK. Thanks.'

'Coffee-bar on the ground floor. Better than the ward machine,' he said. 'They do take-away.'

'Do you want me to bring you anything back?'

He shook his head. 'Caffeine, right now, would blow my head off.'

'I won't be long,' she promised.

The coffee-bar did a selection of tempting-looking cakes, including slices of Grasmere gingerbread and Westmorland pepper cake, but Mallory resisted the temptation, sticking to just a double espresso. By the time she got back to the ward, Will had fallen asleep.

She smiled ruefully—maybe their conversation just wasn't meant to be—and quietly gathered her belongings together. She was about to tiptoe out of the cubicle when a husky voice demanded, 'Where're you going?'

Mallory nearly dropped her coffee. 'I thought you were asleep!'

'Just resting my eyes,' He mumbled. 'Sit. So, what're you doing in the Lakes in January? Not th' right time year f' holiday.'

'Will, you're so tired, you're slurring your words. You need to rest.' She froze. 'Unless you're reacting to the co-proxamol.'

'Neither. Talk to me,' he insisted.

Mallory sighed. 'I just need space to think,' she said simply, dropping her rucksack and waterproof next to the chair and sitting down. 'Make some decisions.'

'Such as?' he prompted.

This was it. The big one. Could she tell him?

But he was a stranger. Someone who wasn't involved. Someone who might help her see a way through this whole mess. 'Whether I'm cut out for a career in medicine. I thought maybe I'd done the wrong thing.' How could she possibly stay on as a GP after what had happened? But, on the other hand, how could she break her father's heart by giving up medicine? Whatever she did would be wrong.

'Did all the right things with me,' Will said. 'Checked my pupils, kept me talking—till I passed out on you— double-checked the painkillers.'

'Yes.' She bit her lip. 'When I saw the accident happen, my instincts took over. So maybe it's a sign that I shouldn't give up just yet.'

'What made you think that you should?'

She stared into her coffee. 'Because I nearly killed some-one.'

CHAPTER TWO

THERE was a long, long pause. A pause in which Mallory couldn't bring herself to look back at Will. A pause that seemed to last for hours, though it could only have been seconds.

'What happened?'

His voice was gentle. Kind, not condemning. She glanced up at him and saw only concern in his eyes, not judgement. And then, at last, she was able to tell him.

'One of my patients came in complaining of a sore shoulder.' Mallory swallowed. 'Lindy had been carrying her toddler about, so I just assumed it was a muscle sprain. I should have thought about shoulder-tip pain being caused by irritation of the diaphragm.'

Will clearly followed her train of thought, as he said, 'Did she say she was pregnant?'

Mallory bit her lip. 'No. She said she was on the Pill, and she'd had a light period a couple of weeks before. I should have known better. As a doctor, I know that you can still have vaginal bleeding in pregnancy, and if she'd missed a pill or had been ill, her contraceptive might have let her down. But I didn't push it.' She took a swig of coffee.

'Ectopic pregnancy?' Will guessed.

'Yes. And I didn't pick it up. I was her GP, and I let her down. Badly. I didn't give her a pregnancy test, just in case, and I didn't send her for a scan. If I had, they'd have picked it up early enough.'

'Any abdominal pain?'

'No.'

Will shrugged. 'Hard one to call if she said she wasn't pregnant, had no abdominal pain.' He swallowed hard.

Clearly he needed a drink, Mallory thought. How could she be so selfish as to sit here and jabber on at him, burden him with her problems, when he really needed looking after? She put her coffee on his bedside cabinet and brought the cup of water down within his reach.

'Thanks.' He took a small sip through the straw, then another. Then stopped. 'Don't want you to tell me off again,' he said.

That half-smile again. She'd bet her last penny that the full monty was the type of smile that would make you cross frozen wastes. Correction. The type of smile that would make frozen wastes feel like lush, temperate pastureland. 'One in five.'

'Hmm?' She'd lost him completely.

'One in five. Women with ectopic pregnancy who have normal periods.'

She knew the statistic too, but it didn't make her feel any better.

'But I should have checked, Will. I didn't.'

Because she'd been too preoccupied with Geoff. Kind, sweet Geoff and his completely unexpected proposal. Well, it hadn't been that unexpected—she'd known from the start that his feelings had been stronger than hers. She'd known what the right answer should have been, but had asked him for time to think about it. Think about whether she could settle down at the practice in the New Forest, bury her love for the mountains and become the domesticated doctor he'd wanted her to be; whether she could live someone else's dreams for the rest of her life. Or whether she could bring herself to hurt him by saying no.

In the end, there had been only one decision. The kindest thing for both of them. She'd told him she loved him, but she couldn't be the woman he needed. She couldn't be his wife. She'd written out her resignation and applied to register as a locum in Cumbria—putting distance between them and giving her a chance to climb while she thought about what to do next.

And then, in the grim weeks when she'd worked out her notice, when she'd seen how Geoff had lost weight and she'd had dark shadows under her eyes and had started wondering maybe if she should have just put his happiness before her own and said yes, she'd nearly lost a patient. Lindy. 'Her tube ruptured the next day. She went into shock, lost a lot of blood. They nearly lost her—as it was, the Fallopian tube had to be removed and she needed a lot of transfusions. And it was all my fault. If I'd done my job properly, sent her for a scan, they'd have seen the problem and taken her into surgery before the tube ruptured.'

'You're a doctor—but you're human.' Will reached to take her hand with his uninjured one.

The feel of his skin against hers sent a shiver of sheer pleasure down her spine. She should pull her hand away—right now—but she couldn't.

He squeezed her hand. 'We all make mistakes.'

Not on this scale. All because her mind hadn't been on her job. 'I should have known better. And my incompetence ruined a family's Christmas.' More than one family's, actually. Three. Lindy's, Geoff's and her own.

'Mallory, your patient didn't die.'

'No.'

'Had she already lost a Fallopian tube?'

Mallory shook her head.

'No reason why she can't have a baby in future, then.'

'But it shouldn't have happened in the first place,' Mallory insisted obstinately.

'Your senior partner gave you time off?'

'I resigned,' she said quietly. What else could she have done? She'd let everyone down. Charles—Geoff's father, the senior partner and her father's best friend from medical school, the man who'd given her the job in the first place. Her own father, who'd so wanted her to follow in his footsteps. Geoff, who'd wanted her to be his wife and the mother of his children.

'Why?'

Because of Geoff. Though she couldn't tell Will that. And then, after what happened with Lindy... 'Maybe I'm just not meant to be a doctor,' she said. She bit her lip. 'Dad's a GP. So are my brothers—they work in the same practice, actually. So right from the start everyone assumed I'd do the same. The only thing I did differently was to work in another practice when I qualified—Dad thought I was just gaining experience until I was ready to join Drs Ryman, Ryman and Ryman. But I screwed it up and I let everyone down.'

'You're being too hard on yourself.'

'Am I?' Mallory shrugged. 'I dunno. I needed time to think. So I came here.' She smiled wryly. 'I suppose I take after my mother. When in doubt, go climbing.'

'So what are you going to do?'

'Climb. Think about what I want to do.'

Will's hand tightened on hers for a moment, and then he moved his hand away. And he'd gone pale. 'Are you all right?' she asked.

'Fine.'

He didn't look it. She placed her hand on his forehead. No temperature. His breathing wasn't rapid or shallow. She swiftly checked his pulse. A bit fast, but in the normal range. Maybe he was just tired—though she'd tell the nurse on her way out. It might be the first signs of shock. 'Will, I'd better let you rest.'

He shook his head. ''M fine. What're your choices?'

'Give up medicine. Or if I do stay in medicine...I might

do some locuming for a bit. Maybe join Médicins Sans Frontières.'

Her father had accused her of running away. Though how could she have stayed in the New Forest? Mallory had let Charles down on all fronts. Professionally, she'd made a stupid—nearly fatal—mistake. Personally, she'd let his son fall in love with her and had broken his heart—because Mallory knew that she couldn't marry Geoff. She loved him dearly, but just as a friend—she wasn't in love with him. Geoff was good and kind and honest and decent, and he'd make somebody a fantastic husband. He'd be a brilliant dad. But he wasn't the right one for her. Climbing in extreme conditions was as alien to him as the planet Mars. The one time she'd confessed to Geoff that her secret dream was to climb Everest, he'd thought she was joking.

Coming to the Lakes had been the right thing to do. A clean break—kinder to Geoff, too, because it would give him the chance to meet someone who deserved him. Someone who'd give him the cosy domestic set-up that was *his* dream.

Not that it had been easy to explain to her father. Dominic Ryman had been delighted when Mallory had told him she was going out with Geoff. A marriage between the two families would have been perfect in his eyes.

But it wasn't going to happen.

Climbing—a chance to think. Will knew someone else who'd taken that point of view. Two people, in fact. One of them was dead and the other was hundreds of miles away in a war zone, working for Médicins Sans Frontières. Just as Mallory could be doing shortly.

And it was all his fault. He had to live with the guilt for the rest of his life. If he'd been different, been a daredevil risk-taking climber like Roly instead of the sort who double-checked all his equipment and never took risks... But he wasn't. And his fiancée Julie had fallen out of love with him and in love with his twin brother.

The night Roly and Julie had told him about their love affair, Will had switched his mobile phone off, taken his phone off the hook and tried to drown his sorrows—knowing that he wasn't on call that night or over the weekend, so he wouldn't be letting his patients down. But he'd been in no mood to think about the weather. He hadn't even realised how bad the storm had got. The mountain rescue team hadn't been able to get in touch with him. But they *had* managed to contact Roly. So Roly had been the one abseiling down the cliff to rescue the stupid, irresponsible, *brainless* climber who'd decided to tackle Sharp Edge— the scariest slopes in the Lakes—in appalling weather and had got stuck.

If he himself hadn't been so selfish, trying to blot out his feeling of misery and betrayal, *he* would have been the one who'd answered the call. *He* would have been the one who'd plummeted down the cliff when the rope had snapped. Roly would still be alive, and Julie wouldn't be nursing a broken heart. She wouldn't be feeling so miserable without the love of her life that she'd be risking her own life in a war zone, because nothing mattered to her any more…

He pulled his thoughts away with difficulty. This wasn't about him. It was about Mallory. Mallory, the stranger who'd come to his rescue at the accident and who even now was keeping him company when she owed him absolutely nothing.

Mallory, who was a trained GP.

And, like it or not, he had problems of his own to face as well. Such as who was going to replace him until he was fit enough to work again.

'I might have a solution,' Will said slowly. To both their situations.

She frowned. 'What?'

'Look at me.' He gestured to himself. 'I'm a GP. But I can't see my patients from a hospital bed. And I'm left-handed.' He gave his cast a rueful look. 'Can't update patient notes, can't write out a prescription—can't even sign one printed off the computer. Or drive out to house calls.'

'I think driving's out for a few weeks.'

She smiled. And it transformed her face so much he almost wished he hadn't made her smile. Because it was like being a child with his nose pressed against the toyshop window, longing for something he couldn't have.

'Look, you need some space to think, a chance to see if you still want to work as a doctor, but without any pressure. I need a locum. And I really hate interviewing. Interviewing with a headache's going to be even worse. So if you agree to be my locum, we could solve each other's problems.'

She frowned. 'But I've just told you. I nearly killed someone.'

'You made a mistake—a mistake that anyone could have made in the circumstances,' he corrected. 'And you've already shown me that you've learned from it. Look at the way you double-checked whether I'd had a previous bad reaction to co-proxamol.'

'Ye-es.'

Co-proxamol, which had taken away the pain. At least he could think clearly again. He wasn't slurring any more either. And hopefully his mouth was working in synch with his brain again and he sounded coherent. Because he really, really needed to talk Mallory round to his way of thinking. 'Everyone doubts themselves at some point. If a patient dies on you, you always think it's your fault—that maybe you could have saved them if only you'd done something else, tried another drug or referred them for a different procedure.'

'That's different. It's not the same as making a stupid mistake in the first place.'

'A mistake that you won't repeat. Don't be so hard on yourself,' Will said softly. 'Everyone deserves a second chance.'

'Can't the others at your practice cover you?'

'They've probably taken care of my list for today, they'll manage tomorrow and it's not my weekend on call anyway,' Will said, 'but it wouldn't be fair of me to ask for more. I need a locum, starting Monday. It's going to take—what, six weeks?—until my arm's out of plaster, and who knows how long before my leg's right again? Three months?'

'Not to mention the physio you'll need to stop your muscles atrophying. And remember, no weight on that leg—you don't want to risk malunion. It's the most common problem with a fractured tibia.'

He nodded. 'See? You *think* like a doctor, Mallory.'

'Maybe.'

'Even if it's only for a month, it'll take the pressure off my partners,' Will said.

'And what will your senior partner have to say about it?' Mallory persisted.

'He agrees with me.'

She frowned. 'But I'm the only one who's visited you.'

'I'm the senior partner.'

Mallory stared at him. 'Either you're incredibly young to be a senior partner, or you've got a picture in your attic.'

Well, of course he was young. He'd thrown himself into his work since the accident. But Mallory had enough on her plate. He wasn't going to lay his own guilt trip on her. 'Maybe both. I'm thirty-four.'

'What will your partners think when you tell them you've picked a stranger off the streets to be your locum?'

'A qualified doctor,' he corrected, 'who rescued me from

the accident. Siobhan'll say it's fate. She and Tom'll be delighted to have you on board. Nathan—he's my practice manager—will be only too pleased not to have to go through the list of locums and find someone who wants to do more than one morning a week.' He paused. 'Um…you *do* want to do more than one morning a week?'

'Yes. I could do three or four surgeries a week—even five—and still get a chance to explore the area.'

She meant 'climb'. He forced himself to ignore the ache in his heart. 'So. You're a qualified GP. Vocational training up to date?'

She nodded. 'And I've got certificates to prove it.'

'Fully insured?'

'Yes. I've got the papers, too.'

'You're MRCGP?'

'Yes, I'm a Member of the Royal College of General Practitioners.' She smiled. 'OK, now I believe you're an extremely young senior partner.'

'Huh?' He didn't follow.

'If you can remember to ask all the right screening questions when you've been hit by a car, you've been in Theatre and you're on painkillers…' She spread her hands. 'You'll be seriously scary when you're back on your feet.'

'I'm not scary in the slightest.' He gave her a wicked look. 'Though Marion is.'

'Marion?'

'Marion Prentiss, our receptionist—she's one of the old school and a complete dragon.'

'Bit stereotypical, isn't it?'

He shrugged. 'But it works. Nobody misses an appointment at our practice, believe you me. And God help the doctor who's late for surgery. Though if you're ill, the first one to be there offering help is our Marion. She's a pussycat really—you just have to know how to treat her.'

'So what's the secret?'

'Make sure you're on time—and make her a cup of coffee when you get in. Then there's Hayley, our practice
nurse, the type who's everyone's favourite aunty. They're
a good team.'

'I need time to think about it,' she warned.

'Of course you do.' But there was still something that
could put a major spanner in the works. 'Are you registered
up here?'

Mallory nodded. 'I registered a while back, when I resigned from my last practice. I knew I wanted to stay in
Cumbria for a few months and my savings weren't going
to keep me indefinitely. I had the official acceptance
through before Christmas—though I was planning to do
some climbing before putting my name down on the lists
or joining the local association of non-principals.'

'So the paperwork's not going to be a problem.' Will
knew it could take over a month to sort out registration. At
least he didn't have to face that hurdle. 'Good. Go and think
about it. Have a look round the surgery in Darrowthwaite
tomorrow, meet the gang, see if you like them—I'm sure
they'll like you. If you agree to join us for a while, Nathan
can sort out the contractual side of things and references.'
He paused. 'But if you're going climbing, you *will* tell
someone where you're going and when you'll be back,
won't you?'

She gave him a withering look. 'Of course. I've been
climbing for over twenty years, I'll have you know.'

'What was that you were saying about pictures in the
attic?' he teased.

'I started young. Mum's always been mountain-mad—I
was named after the Everest climber George Mallory,' she
said. 'My brothers and I were climbing almost before we
could walk.'

She didn't mention her father, he noticed.

'So I'm perfectly aware of the drill—and that if you have

to call the rescue services from your mobile phone, tell them you're in the Lakes because at the top of Scafell you might get connected to the services in Inverness or the Isle of Man.'

'OK.' He lifted his uninjured hand in a gesture of surrender. 'So I was teaching you to suck eggs.'

'I just like the challenge of climbing,' she said. 'Seeing a rockface, getting to the top and knowing that I've beaten all the elements by myself.'

Yeah. Will remembered that feeling. He even missed it. But the last time he'd tried to go climbing, he'd only got as far as pulling his boots on. And then the guilt had slammed in. He couldn't do it any more. He just *couldn't*. 'Mad.'

Her jaw set and he realised he'd spoken aloud. 'I don't take stupid risks,' she informed him tartly.

He hadn't meant *her*. But how could he tell her the truth? 'Sorry. I didn't mean to insult your intelligence.'

'No offence taken.'

'Good.' He made himself say it, even though the words reopened his wounds. 'Go climb your mountain, Mallory.' He couldn't resist adding, 'Safely.'

She gave him a speaking look.

He ignored it. 'And then tell me what you've decided tomorrow.'

'OK. But you need to get some rest.' She gathered her belongings together again and this time, Will didn't protest. 'Is there anyone you want me to ring for you?'

'Thanks, but it's OK. The town grapevine's pretty good. The minute surgery's over, no doubt Nathan will be here.'

'I'll see you tomorrow, then.'

'Yep.' He dredged up another smile, though he was starting to hurt again. 'Have a nice evening.'

'You, too.'

When Mallory closed the cubicle curtain behind her, Will

felt strangely bereft. Disappointed, even. Though, of course, she wasn't going to kiss him goodbye, not even on the cheek. And he had to be off his head, asking her to be his locum without checking first that she really was who she said she was, that she was properly qualified and competent. Especially when she'd already told him she had doubts about staying in medicine. Big doubts.

But there was something about Mallory Ryman.

Oh, who was he trying to kid? Something, indeed. The woman was gorgeous. Drop-dead gorgeous. But he'd spent the last five years following his head instead of his heart. He wasn't going to change that now. If Mallory agreed to be his locum, and *if* her paperwork checked out—he certainly wasn't going to put his patients at risk—they'd be friends. Strictly friends. Nothing more. Because how could he possibly get involved with someone who climbed, when climbing had shattered his life?

CHAPTER THREE

MALLORY reached for the next hold, feeling her muscles stretch. This was what she liked most about climbing, testing her body to its limits and then getting to the top and knowing she'd achieved it all by herself. She tensed and pulled up, then let the crampon do its work and make her toehold safer, before reaching up for the next hold. She liked taking risks, yes, but she always calculated them first. She didn't climb in blizzards or driving rain or when the temperature was below zero and the rocks were covered in black ice—well, not unless she was part of a group, doing something she secretly regarded as training for Everest, her long-held dream. And even then only when she had an ice axe and crampons.

Should she accept Will's offer? And was he right? Did she deserve a second chance? Maybe. If it had happened to someone else, she wouldn't have judged that person too harshly. But she'd prided herself on being the perfect doctor, on never making mistakes. On being good enough to meet the standards her father and brothers had already set.

'Concentrate on the rocks,' she told herself crossly. She had to think about the climbing. If she didn't, she'd slip and fall. She knew the way it worked—she'd done it often enough. Just think about climbing, and let her subconscious go to work on solving her problems. By the time she'd reached the top of Helvellyn, she'd have the answer.

She gave all her attention to the rocks, focusing on the climb, judging each handhold and foothold with a practised eye. When she reached the top, she sat down and looked out over the valleys below her. Ullswater glimmered in the

pale January sun to one side of her, Thirlmere to the other.
It was a beautifully clear day without so much as a hint of
a cloud, so she could see Blencathra in the distance and the
peak at Skiddaw. It was freezing cold. She couldn't feel
the tip of her nose and the exposed part of her face had
probably been whipped red raw by the wind, but she
couldn't help smiling. Because she'd just come home.

Home.

It wasn't really home—she wasn't sure if anywhere was
home right now—but the peaks of Cumbria had called her
north in the dark days before her resignation. And it could
be home, at least for a while, if she acted as Will's locum.

Though Will Cooper was another problem. There was a
definite pull between them. If they'd met in other circumstances… But no. He was in plaster and pins. And that was
enough to keep her common sense working. If she worked
with him—and it was a big if—their relationship would be
strictly business.

Her mobile phone shrilled. She pulled it from her inside
pocket and answered automatically without bothering to
look at the display first. 'Mallory Ryman.'

'Hey, there, Wonder Woman.'

Mallory chuckled. Of all the people she could have done
with talking to right now, her sister-in-law Renee was top
of the list. 'Hey, there, Renny-babes.'

There was a pained sigh. 'Repeat after me. Ruh-*nay*.'

'Ren-nee-ee,' Mallory teased. 'How are you?'

'Fine, honey. And *where* are you?'

'Top of Helvellyn. Views to die for. You'd love it.'

'With all that hard work first? Give me a Jacuzzi any
day!'

Mallory's grin widened. Renee was an unabashed he-
donist. Her suggested solution to Mallory's dilemma had
been to spend a week together at a spa. Flotation tank,

Indian head massage, facial, Jacuzzi, the works. Followed by some serious shopping. 'Spent all Mikey's money yet?'

'I'm working on it,' Renee teased back. 'Seriously, honey, you haven't been in touch for over a week. The menfolk are muttering. And, um, Geoff's been up to see us.'

'Right.' Mallory coughed. 'You didn't tell him where I was?'

'We don't actually *know* where you are, do we, honey? Just that you're somewhere in the Lakes, getting your head together. Anyway, I had a little chat with him. So he knows you're not going to change your mind.'

'Thanks, Renee.'

'And you did the right thing. He's a lovely guy, but he's not the one for you. He's too tame. You need Spiderman.'

'Don't you mean Superman?'

'Nope, I mean Spiderman. You need a climber. Someone who understands why you do what you do—and wants to do it with you.'

'Mikey's a climber and you wouldn't be seen dead in crampons,' Mallory pointed out.

'Yeah, but I understand why he does it. That makes a difference. So, has the climbing helped?'

Mallory sighed. 'Yes and no.'

'Want my take on it?' Without pausing for an answer, Renee continued, 'You're a good doctor, Mallory. You're cutting yourself to pieces over a mistake—but it's the wrong mistake you're focusing on.'

'What do you mean, the wrong mistake?'

'Your patient. It could have happened to Mikey, to Jonno, to your dad. The Rymans aren't perfect. No, honey, your mistake was working too close to home.'

'The New Forest isn't exactly close to Gloucestershire.'

'In the States, honey, that'd be doorstep distance. But that's not what I mean. Charles is your father's best friend, so you were personally involved even before you started seeing Geoff. And I don't think you should come back here and be Doctor and Daughter either. You'd be worrying that the boys would be watching you and judging you all the time. What you need is a fresh start in a practice that isn't linked to your personal life. So you're there on your own merits. And your partners will stay that way—*working* partners.'

'Maybe.' Mallory sighed. 'I can't live off my savings for ever. I've got to get a job at some point.' She grimaced as she remembered the balance that had flashed up when she'd withdrawn some cash earlier that day. 'Sooner rather than later.'

'So get the one you're trained for.'

'I've, um, been offered a locum position.'

'Up there?'

Mallory quickly filled Renee in on the Will situation. 'I told him what happened and he said I needed a second chance.'

'You do,' Renee said emphatically.

'And it solves his problem, too—if I do it, he won't have to worry about finding a locum who'll do the hours he needs.'

'Then go see the practice,' Renee said. 'See what you think. If you like them, give it a try. If it doesn't work out, you can always move on. No one'll think any less of you.'

'I suppose you're right.'

'Course I am, honey. I'm *always* right.' Renee chuckled. 'Let me know how it goes. And I won't breathe a word to the boys. Your mom thinks the same as I do. So you tell them when you're good and ready, OK?'

'OK.'

'You take care, now.'

'You, too. And, Renee?'

'Yeah?'

'Thanks.'

'Any time, honey.'

By the time Mallory had come back down Helvellyn and driven back to Darrowthwaite, it was getting near the end of surgery.

'I'm sorry, neither of the doctors will be able to see you today,' the receptionist told her bluntly. 'Their lists are full.'

Direct. Well, she could cope with that. Mallory smiled and held out her hand. 'You must be Mrs Prentiss.'

The receptionist frowned. 'And you are?'

'Mallory Ryman. I'm not looking for an appointment with one of the GPs, but I would like a quick word with the practice manager, please.'

Mrs Prentiss's lips pursed as she looked Mallory up and down.

'I'm not a drug rep either, Mrs Prentiss, if that's what you're thinking,' Mallory said hastily. 'I was with Dr Cooper at the hospital yesterday.' Coffee. Will had said something about coffee. 'Look, I can see you're busy so I don't want to hold you up, but he asked me to call in and have a quick chat with Nathan. If I…if I get you a cup of coffee, would you be able to see if Nathan can spare me a couple of minutes, please?'

To her surprise, the receptionist burst out laughing. 'Will tell you how to soft-soap me, did he?'

'Er…' Mallory flushed.

'Third door on the right,' Mrs Prentiss said. 'Nathan's expecting you. Helvellyn cold, was it?'

'But good.' Mallory couldn't help smiling back. Will had been spot on about the Darrowthwaite grapevine. 'Thank you.'

Nathan turned out to be tall and thin, with his hair cut short to disguise a thinning patch. 'I'm glad you're here,' he said. 'Will's making my life a misery. He's called me six times today already! Good climb?'

'Yes, thanks.'

'I gather Will's already told you about the practice. So, is there anything you'd like to ask me?'

This was all going way too fast. She hadn't even said yes yet!

'Sorry, I'm bulldozing you.' He smiled at her. 'Let me show you around.'

The place was perfect. Purpose-built, but from traditional materials and designed to fit in with the buildings around it. Four consulting rooms plus the practice nurse's room. 'And this room's for visiting specialists—we have a weekly phlebotomist, osteopath, chiropodist and physiotherapist,' Nathan told her. 'We also have a room for the health visitors and district midwife—they cover three practices between them.'

'It's a good set-up,' Mallory said. Very similar to Charles's practice.

Just as Nathan was showing her back to his office, the doors of the other doctors' surgeries opened simultaneously.

'You must be Mallory. I'm Siobhan Reilly,' the pretty blonde announced, shaking Mallory's hand. 'And this is Tom Fitzgerald.'

Tom, who was small and round and lively, grinned at her. 'And neither of us makes a habit of diving in front of cars, you'll be pleased to know.'

'But that means you'll have to be the practice hero doctor while Will's out of action,' Siobhan informed her. 'Tom can't because he's sleep deprived.'

'Twins. Teething,' he explained. 'And Siobhan can't because she's scared of heights.'

'And you're a climber,' Siobhan said. 'So you've drawn the short straw.'

'Stop bullying the poor girl,' a voice behind them chided. 'Take no notice of them, love. I'm Hayley, the practice nurse. And you two can just leave her alone and get back to your patients.'

'Yes, Aunty Hayley,' the other doctors chorused, laughing.

Clearly Will had been talking about a shared and much-loved joke when he'd referred to the practice nurse as 'favourite aunty'.

'See you later, Mallory,' Siobhan said, and she and Tom returned to their rooms.

'Just popped along to say hello,' Hayley said. 'And to say thanks for looking after our Will for us.'

'Pleasure,' Mallory said.

'When we heard about the accident, we couldn't believe it. It just didn't seem fair, after the last one. But at least he's all right. Thanks to you.'

'I didn't do a lot,' Mallory said honestly. 'Just tried to keep him conscious while we waited for the ambulance.' And what did Hayley mean, 'after the last one'? Was this the second time Will had been hit by a car?

'I'll leave you to it,' Hayley told her with a smile. 'I've got two tetanus jabs waiting, and if I leave them any longer they'll have scared themselves into going home again.'

After such a welcome, Mallory could only do one thing. Take Renee's advice. 'About these questions,' she said to Nathan.

Nathan nodded. 'Fire away.'

'Would you like to see my certificates and CV?' Then she chuckled. 'And don't tell Will. I want to do it myself.'

'That's the least he deserves for pestering me!' Nathan told her.

'Come and sit down. Good climb?' Will asked when Mallory put her head round the curtain of his cubicle.

'Yes, thanks. I brought you some grapes.' She opened the bag for him, then put the grapes on the table that swung over his bed so he could reach them. 'Seedless. And I washed them first.'

'Thanks. Did you go to see Nathan?'

'Didn't Nathan tell you?'

'He didn't tell me anything,' Will complained.

She put him out of his misery. 'Yes. I saw him.'

'And?'

She handed him an envelope.

'What's this?'

'My references,' she said simply. 'You'd better check me out properly if you want me to take this job.'

'You'll do it, then?'

She nodded. 'Until you're better, but I'd prefer it to be on a trial basis. Give it a week, see if we suit each other.'

'Fair enough.'

'Once you've checked out my references.'

'Have you given a copy to Nathan?'

'Yes. Along with all the necessary papers.'

'Then he'll already have it in hand.' He gave her another of those half-smiles. She'd been expecting the full wattage but, then again, he *had* just been hit by a car. A half-smile was probably as much as he could manage. 'Welcome aboard Darrowthwaite Surgery. Now, can you do me another favour?'

'Such as?'

He dropped his voice to a whisper. 'Get me out of here! I can't stand another night of noise and clattering.'

'Will, you've got an internal fixation and an arm in plaster. How are you going to manage at home?'

'The cottage has a downstairs bathroom and there's a sofa bed in the living room. I'll cope.'

'What do the doctors say?'

'Is he still on about discharging himself?' a voice enquired. 'Honestly, medical staff really are the worst patients. Demand to see their notes, want to know why you're still doing their obs when they feel perfectly well, and say they're going home well before they're actually ready.' The staff nurse swiftly took Will's temperature and checked his pulse.

'Apyrexial, pulse normal, no sign of nausea, no unusual pain, and if you check under the dressing there won't be any signs of infection. No redness, no heat, no sign of pus.' Will ticked the list off on the fingers of his uninjured hand. 'Now, can I go home?'

'You know what the doctor said,' the nurse told him gently as she wrote up his chart. 'Only on condition you have someone to look after you.'

'You're in the best place,' Mallory added.

'Then I'll get a taxi and discharge myself,' Will said.

'Talk some sense into your boyfriend, will you? Please?' the nurse teased.

Mallory flushed deeply as the nurse left. She wasn't Will's girlfriend—just his locum. But if the nursing staff thought that, no doubt Will's partners and patients would think she was trying to come on to him… And what would his *real* girlfriend think?

'What about your wife—your girlfriend?' Mallory asked. 'How does she feel about this?'

'I'm single,' Will said, his voice suddenly crisp, 'and I like it that way.'

Ouch. She'd definitely trodden on sore toes there. It sounded as if he'd recently split up with someone. 'Your mum?'

Will groaned. 'Please, no. It was bad enough when I rang her earlier to tell her about the accident. Especially after—'

He stopped abruptly, and Mallory wondered what he'd been going to say.

'Look, I can manage. Mrs Hammond'll come in a couple of times a week to do my cleaning. If I ask her nicely, she'll pop in to give me some food once a day and do the washing and what have you. All I need's a garden chair or something in the bathroom and I'll be set up perfectly.'

'It's still a risk,' Mallory said.

'I really, really *can't* stay here much longer. It's driving me bananas,' Will said between gritted teeth. 'Now the other patients know I'm a doctor, they're telling me all their ills and asking what they should do—it's worse than being at a party and having everyone demand an opinion on every little niggle!' His half-smile took the edge off his words, but only just. He paused. 'I know you said you were planning on being a locum for a while…have you got digs lined up?'

Uh-oh. She had a nasty feeling she knew what was coming. 'I'm staying at The Limes.'

'I've got a better solution,' Will said. 'My spare room. If you stay at the cottage, there'll be a doctor on the premises if I get into trouble, so they'll let me out.'

Yeah, right.

He grimaced. 'Mallory, this wasn't—isn't—an attempt to seduce you. Sharing my cottage until I'm fit again doesn't mean I'm expecting you to share my bed or anything like that.'

Her skin heated again. She hadn't been thinking along those lines at all. Although now he'd mentioned it… No. He might be drop-dead gorgeous beneath the bruising and the plaster, but she *wasn't* going to have an affair with Will Cooper. She was going to be sensible this time round, and make sure her working partnerships stayed that way. Work only. 'I didn't think you were.'

'What, then?'

'I don't follow.'

'You looked incredibly disapproving,' he said.

'Not disapproving… Just that I hope you don't expect me to be, well, domesticated.'

'Explain.'

'I don't do housework,' she said quietly.

'You don't have to. Mrs Hammond does for me,' he reminded her.

'I don't do cooking either.'

He raised an eyebrow. 'Dare I ask what you *do* do?'

'Cattle-herding and sheep-shearing—I did them both in Australia in my gap year. Mountaineering—I'm a qualified climber. But cooking and cleaning and laundry, no chance.'

'That's fine by me. We'll live on fish and chips and pizza. Just get me out of here.'

She sighed. 'OK. I'll ask if you can go home tomorrow.'

'*Today*,' he said. 'Please, Mallory?'

When he asked so nicely, how could she possibly resist?

'Tomorrow,' Mallory reported back a few minutes later.

'Tomorrow?' Will echoed in horror.

'You can go home after the doctors' rounds, *if* they're happy with your condition. And they won't budge on that. So unless you have any strings you can pull—and pull fast—you're staying put tonight.'

He shook his head. 'But I feel better. Really, I do. I promise to do all my physio, to…to…'

'Will, you were knocked over by a car yesterday morning.'

'But it wasn't at high speed. The driver nearly managed an emergency stop.'

'"Nearly" being the operative word. The car hit you. Be *sensible*.'

Sensible? He nearly laughed. If only she knew… 'All right. But tomorrow's as much as I can take. Anyway, I suppose you need some time to settle in yourself. My keys are in the cabinet there—the one with the insulation tape round it's the front door key.'

'Insulation tape?'

'Quickest way to tell the difference between the front and back door keys. They look pretty much the same,' he explained. 'I'll sort out my spare set for you when I get home.'

'This is a hell of a risk,' she said. 'You don't know me. For all you know, I could be spinning you a line about working as a GP—I could be a thief or even an axe-murderer.'

He lifted his uninjured hand, spreading the palm in the age-old 'so what?' gesture. 'If it means you get me out of here tomorrow, be my guest. Sell the stereo, take the family silver, do what you like. Just get me *out* of here.'

'Be serious, Will.'

'I trust you, Mallory,' he said. 'You didn't have to tell me about what happened with Lindy, but you were honest about it. I knew about it before I offered you the job. And if there was anything else remotely dodgy about you, Nathan would have found out by now and told me.'

'Do you always make decisions this quickly?' Mallory asked.

No. He didn't. He always thought things through before acting, and look what that had got him. Maybe it was crazy, asking a woman he didn't really know to share his house, but then again maybe it was time he took some risks.

'Yes.' Though it wasn't a complete lie. It was true for now. 'Keys,' he reminded her.

She took the bunch of keys from his cupboard.

'Stay there tonight if you like. Did you tell The Limes how long you were staying?'

Mallory shook her head.

'Get them to bill me for tonight. And then tomorrow you can pick…' He stopped. He was rushing ahead of himself, making assumptions. 'I never thought to ask you. Did you come by car or train? No, scrub that. I don't even know if you can drive.'

'I can, and my car's in the hospital car park right now,' Mallory told him with a smile.

Will sagged back against his pillows, relieved. 'Good. Then tomorrow, Dr Ryman, you can rescue me.'

CHAPTER FOUR

MALLORY checked out of The Limes that evening and settled into Will's cottage. It was small and functional—and it had no feminine touches, so clearly he hadn't been living with the girl who'd hurt him. There weren't any photographs to give her a clue either. The only three in evidence were one of a couple she assumed to be Will's parents, one of a brown and white Border collie, and one of Will with another man. A man who looked so like him—albeit blond—that he had to be Will's brother. Both of them were smiling. Will's full-wattage smile was even more breathtaking than she'd guessed it might be.

And then she noticed where they were. At the top of a mountain.

If Will was a climber, why had he made such a fuss about safety? And a keen climber who was about to have an enforced lay-off would surely have made some remark about wishing they could change places. She certainly would have done.

Something didn't quite add up.

She shook herself—it was none of her business—and familiarised herself with the rest of the cottage. The kitchen-cum-dining room was again basic but functional—there was bread in the bread-bin, cheese and butter and milk in the fridge, a bowl of fruit in the middle of the scrubbed pine table and the wine-rack was half-full. She pulled one or two bottles out to look at the labels. It didn't look as if Will drank a lot—but what he did drink was good stuff. Very good stuff, she thought. This was a man with definite tastes. Good taste.

His living room was filled with books and CDs—there wasn't a television, she noted, though the hi-fi system was a seriously expensive make—and his bathroom was spartan but the water was hot and plentiful. He wouldn't be able to have a bath until his leg had healed a bit more, but he could probably manage a shower. Though he'd need a plastic garden chair to sit on so he didn't have to balance precariously on one leg. From the little she'd seen of him, she guessed that losing his independence would be the worst thing for Will.

His small garden contained a tiny shed which was just large enough to store a lawnmower and a minimal collection of tools, but held no garden furniture. The garage didn't yield anything either. Clearly gardening wasn't one of Will's interests. Though a trip to the local DIY superstore netted her a sturdy plastic chair that just about fitted in the shower.

She slept well for the first time in weeks, and Will was waiting impatiently for her the next morning, dressed and ready to go. He was actually drumming the fingers of his free hand on the table, she noted with amusement. And someone had clearly given him a shave. Will Cooper scrubbed up very nicely indeed.

Not that she should be thinking about him in that way. Renee was absolutely right. She needed a fresh start where her work wasn't linked to her personal life. Falling for her new boss would be a complete no-no.

'I've been waiting for *ages*. I thought you'd never get here,' Will complained.

'There's no point in being here at eight if the rounds don't finish until eleven,' she said sweetly. 'Thank you, Mallory, for coming to pick me up.'

'Thank you, Mallory,' he repeated, flushing at her gentle rebuke.

She grinned. 'Come on, oh grumpy boss. Let's get you home.'

Then she realised what she'd said. Home. As if it were *their* home. Hadn't she already been through why they weren't and never could be a couple? Hopefully he'd take it as meaning just *his* home.

She wheeled him out to her car and together they managed to cram him into the passenger seat of her small Renault.

'I'll have to get you insured to drive my car,' Will said as she drove them back to Darrowthwaite.

'Why?'

'If we get bad weather and you have to do a house call, you'll need a four-wheel-drive. The roads round here can get pretty icy,' he told her.

'Whatever.' She wasn't precious about always using her car. And it would be the sensible thing to do. 'I've got my driving licence with me so you can fax it to the insurance company if you need to.'

'Good. Sounds as if we're on the same wavelength.' He gave her a half-smile that made her feel all shivery inside. She just about managed to force herself to concentrate on the road instead.

When they arrived at his cottage, it took a while to manoeuvre him out of her car. She hadn't thought to borrow a wheelchair so she had to help him with his crutches. But eventually they made it, and Will groaned in relief as he sank onto the sofa. 'I could really do with a glass of wine after that. A nice cold Chablis.'

'Not with co-proxamol,' she said crisply.

His face mirrored his disgust. 'That's the one bad thing about sharing a house with another doctor. You know as much as I do,' he complained.

'You can have tea—or tea.'

'Coffee?' he tried. 'Please?'

'As you've asked nicely,' she deadpanned.

She came back a few minutes later with a tray of coffee and cake.

Will perked up. 'Proper coffee? I thought you didn't do cooking?'

'This isn't cooking. It's a necessity,' she said, depressing the plunger on the cafetière and pouring the hot liquid into two mugs. 'Milk? Sugar?'

'Neither, thanks.'

'That's easy, then.'

'Mmm, and that's nice,' he said after his first sip. 'Lucky guess or did someone tell you?'

'What?'

'Maple pecan's my favourite.'

She smiled. 'Neither. It's mine.'

He looked at the tray. 'Gingerbread, too. Better and better. All you have to do now is tell me you like anchovies on pizza and you'll be the perfect housemate.'

'I *detest* anchovies,' she said feelingly.

'Win some, lose some.' He took another sip of coffee. 'Seriously, Mallory, I appreciate you rescuing me. For the second time.'

'Just don't make a habit of it,' she said lightly.

'I'll try.' He paused. 'So…what made you choose the New Forest?'

She nearly dropped her coffee. 'What?'

'You love mountains. And you can't get much further from good climbing areas than the New Forest. Why not Wales, or Derbyshire, or Scotland, or here?'

She was silent for a long time. But he was a skilled doctor and she recognised how good he was at using the doctor's greatest weapon. Patience. In the end, she decided to give in. Tell him. 'Charles was my dad's best friend at medical school. He offered me a job in his practice. He thought it'd be better for me to get some experience in another practice rather than going straight to join my dad and brothers. And it seemed like a good idea at the time.'

'Probably was.' He looked at her. 'So what happened to your climbing?'

'There was a climbing wall at one of the sports centres nearby, and I spent my weekends here or in Derbyshire. I had a couple of weeks in the Rockies one summer.' She smiled. 'And I did the Three Peaks challenge—Ben Nevis, Scafell and Snowdonia. Charles, bless him, let me have the time off without having to use my holiday entitlement, because I was raising money for a local charity.'

'But?'

She stared into her coffee. 'I think I would have had to leave anyway. Even without the Lindy situation.'

'Because you need the mountains.'

That, and because of Geoff. Not that she could tell Will about him. Even the thought of Geoff made her feel guilty. 'Well. Maybe I'll climb Everest one day. Though competition's tough for places on an expedition.'

'If it's what you really want, go for it.'

There was a strange, shuttered look on Will's face—a look she couldn't interpret. What had she said to upset him? Had the woman who'd broken his heart gone on an expedition and not come back? Had that been the accident Hayley had mentioned—had Will been on the same expedition and felt bad because he'd been the one to come back and his girlfriend hadn't?

But she couldn't ask him straight out, not without being nosy or rude, and if his girlfriend had died she didn't want to rub salt into his wounds.

Mallory took a sip of coffee and changed the subject. 'Actually, I wanted to talk to you about Monday's surgery.'

'It starts at half past eight. There's a practice meeting on Monday afternoons, too. Then house calls, if that's OK?'

'Ye-es. I was just wondering...would you like to sit in on my first surgery? If you feel up to it, of course.'

He frowned. 'Why? Your details checked out. Actually, I spoke to Charles myself this morning. Before you came to pick me up.'

Her eyes widened. 'What did he say?'

'You're a good doctor but you need to sort your life out.'

Had Charles told him about Geoff? Was this Will's way of telling her he knew all about it? 'Sort my life out,' she echoed nervously.

'And trust your own judgement.'

'So he told you about Lindy.'

Will shook his head. 'I told him what you'd told me. And he said the same thing that I did—it was an honest mistake, it could have happened to anyone and you shouldn't give up medicine over it.' He raised an eyebrow. 'He also said he thought you'd be happier up here, and said we should fine you twenty pence for every time you mention the c-word. Or the m-word.'

Mallory relaxed again. So Charles hadn't mentioned how nearly she'd been his daughter-in-law. Or maybe Charles hadn't thought she was right for Geoff either, but hadn't wanted to interfere in his son's life. 'They used to do that at the practice, and buy cream cakes for everyone on a Friday with the proceeds,' she said wryly. 'And if there wasn't enough in the kitty, they'd start asking questions where I'd *have* to answer "climb" or "mountain"!'

'Noted. I'll get Marion onto it,' Will said dryly. She wasn't sure whether he was joking or not until he added, still straight-faced, 'And bearing in mind where we are, I'd say it'll be more like two rounds of cream cakes a week.'

'Meanie,' she retorted, smiling back. 'Seriously, Will, I'd be happier if you sat in. Just so you can see whether I'm good enough to fill in for you.'

'Mallory, I have every faith in you. You just need to get

your confidence back. But if it makes you happier, of course I'll sit in,' he said.

The weekend went incredibly quickly. Will was a good host, with charming manners, though Mallory noticed that he rarely smiled, and never properly—not like in that photograph. And it wasn't just post-accident pain, she was sure. Every so often he'd simply clam up. He'd get this intense, brooding look that told her very clearly to back off, so she didn't push it. Though she couldn't quite put her finger on what she might have said to upset him. Or why he didn't smile.

At least he'd meant it about not expecting her to be domesticated. He'd even suggested that they should work their way through every take-away in the high street, one by one—and, even better, put the washing-up straight in the dishwasher. The cottage might be small and spartan in most respects, but Will had the mod cons that really mattered. Not to mention the fact that he lived near a superb pizzeria.

She spent Sunday on Scafell—after making Will promise he'd ring on her mobile phone if he needed anything—and walked her demons off. And before she knew it, it was half past eight on Monday morning. Will was in the consulting room beside her, propped in a chair with his crutches close to hand. He'd just had time to show her where he kept everything, and it was time to face her first patient.

Her first patient since Lindy had been hospitalised...

'This is Craig Clarke and his mother Rita,' Will said. 'Rita, Craig, this is Dr Mallory Ryman—she's standing in for me for a while.'

'Nice to meet you,' Rita said. 'First on the scene when Dr Will rescued Kelly, weren't you?'

'Something like that.' Mallory smiled back at her. No doubt the Darrowthwaite grapevine knew that she was

Will's house guest, too. There had been half a dozen visitors over the weekend, all bearing fruit or home-made cakes or chocolates for their 'Dr Will'. And the amount of get-well-soon cards and pictures waiting for him at the surgery, drawn by his younger patients, had to be seen to be believed. Will was clearly popular with his patients. 'So what's up with you, Craig?'

The small boy sniffed. 'Mum says she's sick of me having a cold. She says you'll give me some antibiotics,' he finished, 'to make me better.'

'If it's a just cold, antibiotics won't work, I'm afraid,' Mallory said gently. 'How long has Craig had a runny nose, Mrs Clarke?'

'Off and on, as long as I can remember. It's like a constant cold. Sniffles, a cough…'

'Any wheezing?' Mallory asked.

Rita shook her head.

'Is it worse at any particular time?'

'Weekends,' Rita said. 'And at night—he coughs something chronic at night.'

It was beginning to sound more like some kind of allergic illness, Mallory thought. Possibly asthma. 'What do you normally do at the weekends, Craig?'

He shrugged. 'Help Dad with the sheep, play in the barn.'

'Is the barn empty?'

He shook his head. 'No, course not! That's where we keep the hay.'

'And do you play there after school?'

'Sometimes,' he said.

Mallory nodded. Dust, mites, mould—any of them could be the culprits. 'I'd like to listen to your chest, please.' She took a stethoscope from a drawer. 'Could you pull your sweater up for me, please?'

Craig did so, and Mallory listened to him breathe. There

were definite crackles, but no wheezing. 'That's great, sweetheart,' she said. 'Now I want you to play a special game for me—I want you to see how far you can make the arrow on this little tube go.' She took a peak-flow meter from the drawer and showed him how to use it. 'Now take a big breath, and puff as hard as you can!'

He did, and she noted down the measurement—definitely less than she'd expect for a boy of Craig's height. 'And again?' He blew again, then did a third one 'for luck'.

'Is it asthma, Dr Ryman?' Rita Clarke asked.

'It could be—though I'd like to send Craig for a chest X-ray and take a blood sample for some tests, just to make sure. Does anyone in the family have asthma?'

'No.'

'Eczema, or any other sort of allergy?'

Rita shook her head.

'I think he's probably allergic to mould spores in hay— Dr Cooper, wouldn't you agree?' she said.

Will nodded.

Mallory warmed to her theme. 'It's a condition called extrinsic allergic alveolitis or farmer's lung,' she said. 'What happens is that when Craig breathes in the mould spores, his body overreacts to them and the walls of the little air sacs in his lungs get inflamed. It makes it hard for him to breathe—do you get out of breath really quickly if you run, Craig?'

'I hate PE,' Craig said glumly. 'It always makes me cough.'

'We can do something about that,' she said. 'The bad news is, you'll need to find somewhere else to play—or wear a special mask to stop you breathing in the spores. But the good news is…' she turned to Rita '…he's young so we've probably caught it before it really damages his lungs. I'll give him a course of steroids—they're perfectly safe for him to use, and they're not the same kind of thing as body-building steroids,' she explained. 'It'll be a short course, and I'd like him to come back and see me in two weeks. In the meantime, I'll refer him for an X-ray—you should get an appointment through really quickly. And, Craig, I need to pinch just a little bit of your blood.' She turned so he couldn't read her lips, and mouthed at Rita, 'Is he allowed chocolate?' At Rita's nod, she looked at Craig. 'Do you like chocolate, Craig?'

'Oh, yes!' the little boy said.

'Here's the deal. If you let me take a little bit of blood— it's a bit like having an injection and I promise it won't hurt, just feel like a little scratch—I've got some chocolate for you. And a sticker.'

Craig looked slightly dubious, but agreed. Mallory swabbed his inner elbow, then said, 'Oh, did you see that robin at the window?' As soon as the little boy looked away, she had the needle in, and was capping her sample before he'd noticed.

'You were brilliant,' she said, handing him an I WAS BRAVE sticker. 'Now for the chocolate.'

He beamed at her as he took one of the giant chocolate buttons she offered him. 'Thank you, Dr Mallory.'

'Pleasure, sweetheart.' She tapped a prescription into the computer and printed it out. 'Mrs Clarke, I'm giving Craig an inhaler. It's important he uses it regularly—it'll stop the tissues swelling and make it easier for him to breathe. If you're worried about anything, just give me a ring. And if you could come back to see me in two weeks, we'll see how he's getting on.'

'Thanks,' Rita said, and shepherded her son out of the room.

'Why farmer's lung and not asthma?' Will asked.

'No wheezing,' she said simply. 'But the blood test will tell me more—and if the chest X-ray shows mottling, it's

EAA.' She sighed. 'If it is, I hope it hasn't started fibrosing his lungs.'

'He's very young—as you said, we've probably caught it in time,' Will said. 'Good call. If it's asthma rather than EAA, he's on the right medication anyway.'

'Though I'll give them a peak-flow meter and show her how to track the readings if it's asthma,' Mallory added.

'Sounds good to me. And I'll have to remember the robin trick.' Will nodded at her. 'Ready for your next patient?'

'Yup.' She pressed her buzzer to let Marion know she was ready for the next patient.

The morning flew by—and Mallory found herself settling back into the job she'd so nearly given up. By the time she'd seen her last patient, she couldn't believe how late it was!

'OK?' Will asked softly.

She nodded. 'It was easier than I thought. Actually, it reminded me why I chose general practice rather than working in a hospital—you get the chance to follow cases through and build a proper relationship with your patients.'

'Me, too,' he agreed. 'You're a good doctor, Mallory. You just need to get your confidence back and believe in yourself.' He leaned over, lifted his right hand and touched her cheek with the backs of his fingers. It was as if an electric shock coursed through her—she only just stopped herself exclaiming aloud. To her relief, he didn't seem to notice anything. He just told her, 'Have a break. The baker's on the high street does the best baguettes in town. And the staff meeting's at half one in Nathan's office.' And then he hauled himself up on his crutches and left the room.

She stared after him. Why was her mouth tingling like that? He'd merely touched her on the cheek. Not quite impersonal—but not a declaration of love either. Just a kind, friendly gesture to say she'd done well. It was the equivalent of a matey hug, that was all.

Except it hadn't had that effect on her. Oh, no. Her body was reacting as if he'd kissed her. Kissed her properly, demanding a response.

She needed some fresh air. Now. To blow the cobwebs away and the common sense back. Because Will Cooper didn't want to kiss her. And even if he did, it'd be a bad idea. She was his locum, she wasn't staying for long, and she was absolutely not going to mix up her working life and her private life again.

For once, Will was glad of his crutches. Because no way could he have walked out of his consulting room—*Mallory's* consulting room—without help. Why, why, why had he been so stupid as to touch her? Because now he'd felt the softness of her skin, he wanted more. Much more.

Worse, she'd reacted to his touch. She hadn't said a thing—but she hadn't needed to. Her eyes had done it all for her. Her pupils had grown dark and sultry. And her mouth…

It was just as well he was on crutches. Because if he hadn't known about the danger of overbalancing, he would have pulled her into his arms and kissed that beautiful soft mouth. Kissed her until she responded to him, kissed him back, matching his passion with hers.

He groaned. Oh, hell. Right now, he didn't know which was the worse option—being stuck in hospital where he couldn't do a thing, or having to share a house with a woman he wasn't allowed to touch. A woman he most definitely wanted to touch.

Well, he'd just have to keep his libido in check. Mallory was a climber and he'd sworn off mountains for life. He wasn't right for her. And she definitely wasn't right for him. He'd learned from his mistakes with Julie. If he ever fell in love again—which he doubted; he wasn't planning to risk his heart again—he knew it ought to be with a domestic goddess. Someone who'd be there for him, make a fuss over him, let him make a fuss over her. Someone who scented their sheets with lavender and made her own cakes and jam. Someone he could adore and cherish. Someone who wouldn't nag him into climbing again.

Mallory had already told him she wasn't domesticated. Falling for her would be a recipe for disaster.

He just needed to keep remembering that.

CHAPTER FIVE

THE longer Mallory stayed at the practice, the more she felt at home there. As if she'd worked there for her entire life. Siobhan and Tom made her feel as if she were one of the partners, not just a locum filling in for their boss. Marion had accepted her. Hayley mothered her. Nathan was a dream to work with.

The only problem was Will.

Well, he wasn't the problem. *She* was. Her stay in Darrowthwaite was temporary. He wasn't the casual type. So nothing could happen between them. And yet she found herself thinking of him far more than she ought to. Watching him surreptitiously from behind a magazine. Coming up with feeble excuses to spend time with him in the evening, when she really should have let him rest—but, oh, no, she had to have a quick word with him about this patient and that patient and...

Maybe it was time to move on. Before she damaged his life in the same way that she'd damaged Geoff's. Hadn't Will virtually told her that he was recovering from a broken heart? *I'm single and I like it that way.*

A cold shower, Will decided. That was what he needed. He couldn't quite manage a bath, but a shower—that might take his mind off Mallory.

Except it didn't. Because his imagination started supplying all sorts of pictures. Mallory, her soft skin covered in a layer of foam until...

No. He turned the thermostat to ice cold. Ten minutes later, he was just about back in control of his body. That, and a near slip on the linoleum floor when he stepped out of the shower, made him concentrate on something other than his locum. For about thirty seconds.

Yet again he reminded himself that Mallory was his locum. Off limits. And she'd walk out of his life when his arm had healed, in six weeks or so's time.

'You really don't need to come with me on house calls.' Mallory folded her arms and looked at Will. 'You should be resting that leg.'

'I'll be sitting in the car,' he pointed out. 'That's resting.'

'But not with your leg up properly.'

'You don't know the area. It'll be much quicker if I direct you. And I can introduce you to the patients. Some of them can be a bit stubborn with a new doctor.'

'I'm perfectly capable of reading a map.'

He groaned. 'Mallory, if I stay stuck indoors for much longer, I'll go insane.'

'Read a book,' she suggested, not moving a millimetre.

'OK.'

The meekness and suddenness of his agreement made her suspicious. Will wasn't meek in the slightest. He was pig-headed and he liked having his own way. She narrowed her eyes. 'What are you planning?'

He shrugged. 'Not much.'

'Will Cooper, if you're even *thinking* about trying to put weight on that leg…' she warned.

He gave her another of those falsely innocent looks. 'You won't be there to see it, will you?'

'And I won't be there to take you back to hospital so they can patch you up again when you fall over. Did you know that with fractures, the bone most likely to have problems uniting is the tibia?'

'Uh-huh. Apart from the fact you've already told me,

I'm still just about young enough to remember my anatomy lectures.'

'Then stop being so—Ooh! You infuriating man. I'm going to have to take you with me so I don't have to worry about what you're doing,' she growled.

Will raised his right arm in a champion's salute. 'Round one to me.'

'If you didn't have a broken arm,' she threatened, 'I'd…'

She suddenly had a graphic vision of herself wrestling with Will. A fully fit Will who was a good eight inches taller than she was, heavier and had broad shoulders. The kind of muscles that would have her flat on her back within seconds, and…

Oh, no. She definitely shouldn't have let her thoughts stray in *that* direction. Because she could just imagine Will leaning over her, his mouth descending towards hers. His mouth touching hers. Teasing a kiss from her, then another, then unleashing wild—

'Mallory?'

'We're going to be late if you don't get a move on,' she muttered, and went to open the door of his car for him.

Mallory didn't look at him as she helped him into the car. And Will would have paid a large sum of money to know her thoughts during the last couple of minutes. What had made her blush so spectacularly and her pupils darken like that?

Unless her thoughts had taken the same direction as his. A champion celebrating his victory with a kiss.

Maybe this was a bad idea, going on rounds with her. Especially when his knee was only centimetres from hers. She hadn't turned the key in the ignition yet. What if he leaned over and…?

Work, he reminded himself sharply. She's not the one for you.

*   *   *

Their first visit was to Mrs Sherman, an elderly woman in the advanced stages of cancer who'd chosen to stay at home with palliative care, rather than go into a hospice, with the full blessing of her family. Will explained on the way over that Valerie had given up a well-paid job as a solicitor to care for her mother.

'I just want to make Mum more comfortable,' Valerie said when Mallory had checked Mrs Sherman over, given her more painkillers and something for the nausea.

'You're doing an excellent job,' Mallory said. 'Better than the hospice—because she's at home, surrounded by the people she loves.'

'She's my mum.' Tears glinted in Valerie's eyes for a moment. 'She cared for me when I needed it—and now it's my turn to care for her.'

'I'd do the same,' Mallory said softly.

'But her tongue's coated all the time now, and I don't like to keep scraping it—it must hurt. Is there something else I can do?'

'You could try giving her a small chunk of pineapple to chew,' Mallory said. 'The enzyme in pineapple—bromelain—will get rid of the coating. If she can't manage that, small ice chips will help keep her mouth moist, or even a little bit of butter.'

'Butter? I never thought of that.' Valerie gave a tired smile.

'What about you? Are you looking after yourself properly?' Mallory asked gently.

'I'll be fine.'

'Just remember that we're here if you need us,' Mallory said.

'That's what Dr Will always says. To ring him any time of day or night.'

'That goes for me, too,' Mallory said. 'And if you do

need a break—even if it's just for half an hour to go for a walk and get some fresh air—we can arrange some respite care, someone who'll look after your mother for you just for a little while.'

Valerie shook her head. 'She doesn't have much time left. I don't want to look back and wish I hadn't missed a few moments.'

Mallory nodded. 'Sure. But we're here whenever you need us.'

'Thanks.'

Will stayed very quiet on the way to their next patient, merely giving Mallory directions at road junctions. So she'd do the same—give up her job to nurse her sick mother? Which meant what? Either that she was extremely close to her mother, or that she wasn't quite the tough, undomesticated woman she made herself out to be. She'd phoned her parents only once, to his knowledge, since he'd come home from hospital, and she'd switched the subject whenever her family came up.

Definitely deep. But how was he ever going to persuade her to open up to him, show him the *real* Mallory?

Their second visit was to Olivia Hart, a patient with MS. 'It's the remitting form,' Will explained on the way there. 'Her last attack was eight months ago—she's been fine until now, though obviously we're keeping an eye out in case her symptoms start to get worse.'

Mallory nodded. Multiple sclerosis was a difficult disease to forecast. The most common type was the remitting form, where sufferers had one or two attacks a year and were fine in between, but it usually became progressive after about twenty years, where the attacks weren't as frequent or as severe but the patient didn't fully recover between attacks, leading to greater disability.

The disease itself caused damage to the myelin sheath,

the layer of fat around the nerves. It caused scarring which altered the way messages were conducted to and from the brain, so sufferers commonly had muscle problems which affected their ability to move. Fatigue and optic neuritis, which caused temporary colour blindness, loss of vision and eye pain, were other problems.

Will introduced Mallory to Olivia. 'How are you feeling today?' he asked.

'Tired,' Olivia said with a wry smile. 'But we're getting there.'

'Ready for your beta interferon?' Mallory asked. Beta interferon occurred naturally in the body and acted as a chemical messenger. The MS drugs, given by injection, modified the immune system to stop it attacking the myelin sheath.

'Yes. But I know I'll have to come off it if this relapse goes on too long.'

If MS sufferers had two disabling relapses within twelve months, the disability was worse for six months or more and the patient couldn't walk for six months, then the medication had to be discontinued.

Mallory checked her notes swiftly. 'You've got a few months' grace yet.'

'I hope so.' Olivia sighed.

'Any reactions to it?'

'Just the usual,' Olivia said. 'I feel a bit fluey.'

'I think you probably know as much about it as I do,' Mallory said. 'So you know that paracetamol helps with the side effects.'

Olivia nodded. Mallory injected the beta interferon into the muscle and waited until Olivia was comfortable again.

'Anything else you wanted to discuss?' she asked.

'Well... Kevin and I really wanted to start a family. I'm thirty-two. If we leave it much longer...' Olivia's voice faded.

'It's possible for you to have a baby,' Mallory said, 'but you'll have to come off the beta interferon first. Most patients with MS have fewer relapses during pregnancy, but you're more likely to have a relapse in the six months after the birth.'

'Will the baby have MS too?' Olivia asked.

'There's a slight risk,' Mallory said. 'Some studies show that there's a two per cent chance the baby will have it—but that's still very low.' She paused. 'How's the exercise regime coming along?'

'I'm trying,' Olivia said. 'But if I get too hot…'

Mallory nodded in understanding. MS sufferers were more sensitive to changes in temperature and high humidity. If they got too hot it made symptoms worse, particularly fatigue, because the higher the body's temperature, the less the body's nerves could conduct messages from the brain.

'OK. But do what you can,' she said. 'Stay within your limits and try to work it up gradually.'

'I was thinking about trying acupuncture,' Olivia said.

'It does help some people,' Mallory said. 'And you might find that yoga and aromatherapy helps, too—relaxation therapies are good. Some herbal remedies—' She broke off, perplexed, as Olivia started laughing. 'What?'

'Sorry. I should have warned you,' Will said. 'Kevin, um, experimented with growing…oriental tomatoes, let's say. And the local constable would have had to press charges if a message hadn't got here first.'

The penny dropped. 'Cannabis.' Mallory flushed. 'Um, well, I can't suggest something illegal.' Cannabis was still a class B drug and illegal in the UK, although trials were going on in some areas to assess how effective and safe it was in helping muscle stiffness, pain and bladder symptoms in MS sufferers. 'Actually, I meant St John's wort or evening primrose oil.'

Olivia smiled. 'I think you've already made me feel better today!'

A little later, Will and Mallory left, promising to send Olivia more information about acupuncture and aromatherapy.

'I know it's not a scheduled visit,' Will said in the car, 'but we're just around the corner from the Johnsons. Anita Johnson called yesterday because she's worried about her husband—Marion tried to persuade her to bring him in, but he refuses flatly to visit the surgery.'

'Symptoms?'

'Wouldn't give any. But Anita's not a fusspot,' Will said thoughtfully. 'I'd guess it's chest pain or something like that. And his father died young, from liver cancer—so maybe Mark could be worried he has the same symptoms.'

'In which case we need to send him for tests as quickly as possible.'

'Exactly.'

'Or maybe it's something more personal,' Mallory said. 'How old is he?'

'Early fifties.'

'Could be depression. It still has a stigma among the older generation—especially men,' she said. 'And farmers have a higher incidence of depression. Anything else I should know about?'

'One son, one daughter, both work on the farm,' Will said. 'Apart from the usual screening checks and vaccinations, we hardly ever see the family.'

'Right.'

He directed her through a maze of narrow lanes which had no signposts. When they finally drove up a track to Furze End Farm, Mallory realised it would have taken her at least twice as long to find the farm on her own.

She parked as near to the farmhouse door as she could, then helped Will out of the car and grabbed her doctor's bag. Two Border collies met them at the doorway, barking, but instantly shushed at a command from the plump grey-haired woman behind them.

'Sorry about that,' she said. 'Thank you for coming, Dr…?'

'Ryman. Mallory Ryman,' Mallory said, holding out her hand.

'Anita Johnson.' Anita shook her hand warmly. 'And what are you doing out here with those?' Anita asked, turning to Will.

'Checking my locum doesn't frighten my patients away,' Will said lightly.

'Hmm. More like she's keeping an eye on you to make sure you don't go gallivanting around,' Anita said.

'Is Mr Johnson here?' Mallory asked.

'In with the pigs.' Anita flushed. 'I…um…it's a bit personal.'

'Whatever you tell me is in complete confidence,' Mallory said. 'I'm here to help.'

'Me, too,' Will chipped in.

'Would you like a cup of tea?' Anita asked.

Mallory recognised it as a delaying tactic. 'Thanks. That'd be lovely.' She made a fuss of the collies, who'd wormed their way under the table. 'Oh, you soppy pair. You're worse than my aunt's Labradors!'

'If they're bothering you, I'll shut them away,' Anita said.

'No, I love dogs,' Mallory said.

'Daft beggars they are,' Anita said affectionately. 'Never believe one of their brothers is a star on the mountain rescue team.'

Mountain rescue. Now, *there* was a thought. If she stayed…

But she wasn't going to stay. She already knew that.

Then she noticed that Anita was flushing and Will was

looking grim. Was it something to do with the mountain rescue team? Or the dogs? Obviously she couldn't ask Anita now, but maybe later... Besides, she was supposed to be here to see Mark Johnson.

When Anita placed steaming mugs of tea in front of them, Mallory tried again. 'Does Mr Johnson know we're coming?'

Anita nodded. 'That's why he's shut himself in with the pigs. Embarrassed.'

'Whatever it is, I won't laugh, I promise,' Mallory said.

'Well...' Anita's voice dropped to a whisper. 'He never seems to want to...well, have anything to do with me. At night, you know.'

Mallory nodded gravely. Impotence was common enough in Mark Johnson's age group. She could prescribe something to help.

'And he's...well, I think he's *shrinking*,' Anita whispered, her face turning scarlet. 'Down there. That's why he doesn't want me to...you know. I thought he was having an affair—he looked as if he'd been to that sun parlour in Darrowthwaite. But...' She shook her head. 'I don't know.'

'Has he said anything about his heart? Pains in his chest?'

'Now you come to mention it—yes,' Anita said thoughtfully.

Mallory glanced at Will, then back at Anita. 'Did Mark's dad have quite dark skin?'

Anita frowned. 'Yes. Why?'

'And he died of liver cancer, yes?'

Anita nodded. 'Do you think that's what my Mark's got? Liver cancer?'

Mallory shook her head. 'I'll need to examine him, if he'll let me, and send him for some tests, but I think it could be something much more treatable. If I'm right.'

'He won't see you. He says he doesn't need a doctor,' Anita said worriedly.

'But you have a son, yes?'

'David.'

'Does Mark get on well with him?'

'Thinks the world of him.'

Mallory smiled. 'Then I think I know how to talk him round.' She glanced at Will. 'Sounds like haemochromatosis to me. Bronze diabetes.'

'Could be,' Will said thoughtfully.

'Could you show me to the pigs, please, Mrs Johnson?' Mallory asked. Then she turned to Will. 'And you—don't move.' She bent down to the dogs. 'On guard. Don't let him near those crutches, OK?'

Anita took Mallory down the yard to the pigsheds. 'Doctor's here to see you, Mark,' she called. 'Will's locum. You know, the one who saved him and checked over little Kelly.'

'I don't need a doctor,' her husband replied, striding over to the gate. 'I'm sorry, Doc, she's wasted your time.'

'Maybe not. It's about your son,' Mallory said.

'David?' Mark frowned. 'What about him?'

'I think he might have something called haemochromatosis or bronze diabetes,' Mallory said.

'There's nothing wrong with our David.'

'Not yet. But there will be,' Mallory said. 'You see, it's a genetic condition—which means it can be inherited—and it's much more common in men.'

Mark looked suspiciously at her. 'So what does it do, this bronze diabetes?'

Mallory leaned on the gate. 'The body absorbs too much iron. And the excess builds up in the body—in the liver, pancreas, heart, joints and testes. Iron pigment gets deposited under the skin, so he'll turn bronze—as if he's been out in the sun a lot.' Just like Mark, though, given Mark's occupation, his skin colour could simply be from spending so much time outdoors. 'He'll lose his sex drive, his testes will shrink, and if it goes untreated his body won't produce insulin properly and he'll get diabetes. He'll also find his heart will start beating in a funny rhythm, and his liver will get bigger. If it stays untreated, he'll have chronic liver damage—cirrhosis isn't just caused by drinking too much alcohol—and it might lead to liver cancer.'

'Is it curable?' Mark asked anxiously.

'Yes. And the earlier we catch it, the better—in young men, if treated early, we should be able to avoid complications. In an older man who's already developed it, we can make him live a bit longer.' She paused. 'Your father died of liver cancer, didn't he?'

'Yes,' Mark muttered.

'It's possible that he had it. It might have skipped a generation, but the male relatives of sufferers are more likely to have it.'

'How can you find out?'

'A simple blood test,' she said. 'It shows a high level of iron in the blood. If it does, I'd like to send David for a liver biopsy, too—that just means the doctor will take a small sample from his liver. If he's got bronze diabetes, the liver will have iron in it—which it shouldn't.'

Mallory smiled at Mark. 'The best bit's the treatment—all we do is take a bit of blood from a vein twice a week until your iron level's returned to normal, then we might only need to do it four or five times a year.' She paused. 'So, have you been feeling more tired than usual lately, Mr Johnson?'

'It's my age,' he said.

'How about joint pain?' she persisted.

Mark sighed. 'I've got it, haven't I? So I'm going to end up like Dad. And I've done this to my boy.'

'I don't know without examining you and doing a blood

test,' she said gently. 'But if you do have it, you won't necessarily develop cancer of the liver. The earlier we treat it, the less likely it is you'll have a damaged liver.'

'And David?'

'We can screen him, and treat him if he does have the condition,' she said. 'But I do need to test you first.'

He was silent for a long, long time. Finally, he nodded. 'All right.'

'Let's go back to the house,' she said. 'I can examine you in private there, and take a blood sample.'

The examination confirmed her suspicions. His joints were large, too, and when she listened to his heartbeat, she heard a slight arrythmia. She took a sample of blood. 'I'll ring the results through as soon as I get them,' she said. 'I'd like to send you for an ECG—that's an electrocardiogram, where they hook you up to a monitor and print out a trace of what your heart's doing. With luck, we've caught it before your liver's too damaged.'

'I should've come before,' Mark muttered. 'It's just... I dunno. I thought I might have cancer, like my dad. You don't like to think you're going to die before your time. And I thought if I didn't make a fuss, it might go away.'

'It doesn't work like that,' Mallory said softly. 'I'd much rather see a patient who was worried and had a false alarm than see one who'd been worrying for months and turned out to be so seriously ill that I couldn't help.'

'Like rust spots. If you leave them, they get worse and take longer to fix—if you can fix them at all.'

'Exactly. And there was Anita thinking you were having an affair.'

He flushed. 'Of course I'm not. I love her. She's my wife.'

'And she's worried about you, Mark. You need to talk to her.'

He sighed heavily. 'What use am I going to be to her? She needs a proper husband.'

'She's got one,' Mallory said. 'A good one.'

'So, if I have got this bronze diabetes…will what you give me make…?' He coloured even more deeply.

'It should help,' Mallory said gently. 'And there are other treatments that can help with your sex drive.'

'And my boy?'

'We'll check his blood type, too. He might not have it. He might just be a carrier or he might develop the full-blown disease. We won't know until we test your blood, and his,' Mallory explained. 'But the earlier we catch it, the better your chances are.'

'I've been a stubborn old fool.'

She grinned. 'You're not the first and you won't be the last. Buy her some flowers and take her out to dinner.'

'And that's a prescription, Doc?'

'It's a start,' Mallory said.

'I don't know what you said to Mark,' Will informed Mallory on the way home, 'but it worked.'

'I told him I was worried about his son. Explained the whole thing to him—including the symptoms Anita told us he was suffering—and then told him it was genetic. His son might have it and his father probably had it, too. If the blood does show raised iron levels, I think we should test David as well.'

'Agreed,' Will said. 'Good call. I reckon I owe you dinner out.'

'No need. Just doing my job.'

He groaned. 'Oh, please. We're not having pizza *again*, are we?'

'How about Chinese?'

'I fancy a steak. I can't cook it one-handed, and you won't.'

'I warned you, I don't do cooking.'

'Not domesticated in the slightest,' he said softly. More as a warning to himself than anything else.

'And that's the way I'm going to stay.'

CHAPTER SIX

THOUGH Mallory's resolution was severely tested the next morning, when she came downstairs to find Will in the kitchen, scowling into a mirror, a bowl of water on the table in front of him and his face dripping with blood.

'What on *earth* are you doing?' she asked.

'Shaving. What does it look like?' he muttered.

'Messy,' she retorted. 'Will, you're obviously not used to shaving with your other hand. You've cut your face to ribbons. Why don't you use an electric razor?'

His scowl deepened. 'Because I've got sensitive skin, OK?'

That figured. It went with his Celtic good looks.

'And wet shaves don't give me razor burn.'

'Grow a beard, then.'

'Makes my face itch too much.' He rolled his eyes. 'And I wish you hadn't said that word.'

'What?'

'Itch.'

'You said it, not me.'

'My arm's driving me crazy.' He glared at the plaster.

'Someone got out of the wrong side of bed this morning. I'll make us some coffee.' She switched the kettle on. 'OK. Give me the razor.'

'What?'

'I said, give me the razor. I'll do it for you.'

'You might cut me.'

She chuckled. 'Maybe—but not as much as you've already cut yourself. Give.'

70

Will put the razor in her outstretched hand. 'Be gentle with me, Doc,' he deadpanned.

And that was when the trouble started. When he shifted round on his chair, the easiest position for her to shave him was standing between his legs. And she needed to put one hand on his face to make sure he stayed perfectly still while she stroked the razor down over the shaving gel and stubble. She rinsed the blades in the bowl of water and stroked the razor over his skin again.

She didn't look into his eyes. She didn't dare. Because standing this close to him, feeling his skin against her fingertips, was doing strange things to her. Every nerve in her body was aware of him. And not just as her housemate, someone she was helping to shave because his cast stopped him doing a proper job. This was nothing like it had been when she'd shared a house with two women and three men as a medical student. This…was dangerous.

And when she'd stroked the last bit of shaving gel from his skin, wiped his face clean and mopped up the cuts he'd made earlier, Mallory knew she should back away. Right now. So why did her fingertips disobey? Why did they run lightly over his newly smooth skin? Why did her tongue moisten her suddenly dry lips? Why did she look at him? And *why* did she push that lock of floppy hair back over his forehead?

Will's pupils grew huge, and he tipped his head back slightly, offering his mouth to hers. Tempting her. Pleading with his eyes, asking her to kiss him. Beautiful eyes—eyes that made her forget her intention to be sensible. She moistened her lower lip again. Bent towards him. His uninjured arm slid round her back, urging her closer. She touched her mouth to his. Gently, so very gently.

And it was like lighting a firework. The next thing she knew, she was sitting on his lap, her weight on his good leg. Her hands were locked round his neck, her eyes were closed and every sense was filled with Will, from the tingling of every nerve end where his skin touched hers through to the clean, masculine scent filling her nose.

He kissed her back, matching her passion. His free hand slid round to her back, untucked her shirt from the waistband of her trousers and burrowed under the cotton. His fingertips traced tiny circles against her skin, gradually working their way up her spine.

And even though her head was screaming at her to stop, this wasn't a good idea, her body was screaming louder. *Don't you dare stop now!* She wanted more—*needed* more.

Mallory nibbled at Will's lower lip and he opened his mouth, letting her take the initiative to deepen the kiss again. His fingers had just reached the catch of her bra when there was a loud thud, followed swiftly by a metallic snap.

The post.

The noise brought her back to her senses and she jerked away. 'I'm going to be late for surgery.'

'Mallory…'

But she was panicking. Hell, it had been *that* close. Another five minutes and they'd have been making love on the chair. And she'd *sworn* she wouldn't get involved with him. She must have been out of her mind to kiss him like that. 'I'll see you later, OK?'

'OK,' he said. The look on his face said that he wasn't going to let her get away with it that easily, but she restored order to her clothes and left for the surgery.

Mallory was still slightly flustered when she saw her first patient that day. But when Cathy paused on her way out, Mallory realised that she was about to hear the real reason for Cathy's visit rather than the nebulous symptoms of a chest infection.

'I was just wondering… Manic depression. It can pass down the family, can't it?'

'Some scientists think there's a genetic link, but that alone can't cause manic depression—there needs to be some kind of trigger. What makes you think you have it?' Mallory asked gently.

'I… Well, I've just been moody lately. More than usual—like that time of the month, only worse. Half the time I feel like crying.'

'And the other half you're in a whirl?' Mallory asked.

'No.' Cathy sighed. 'I'm not quite as bad as Dad yet. But I remember what he was like years ago. I don't want to end up going the same way.'

'Studies show that most children don't develop the same mental health problem as their parent,' Mallory reassured her. 'And if you do develop it, the good news is that it's controllable.'

'*If* you take your tablets,' Cathy muttered.

Patient compliance was one of the biggest problems with mental illnesses, particularly manic depression, nowadays called bipolar disease. Too many times Mallory had seen patients who stopped taking their medication as soon as they felt well—and their condition had deteriorated fast, so they'd ended up sinking back into depression or swinging into an unsustainable high. Lithium carbonate wasn't a cure, and patients taking it needed their blood levels checking frequently to make sure the levels of lithium weren't too high, but it did help keep the condition under control. 'Doesn't your father take his?'

'He says it's a stigma. I told him no one'll know what you're taking unless you tell them. It could be just an aspirin. But, no, he says everyone'll know and talk about him. He doesn't take the tablets. He tells me he does, but he doesn't. I don't know what he does with them—I think he must put them down the loo or something.' Her face grew pinched. 'And we're the ones who have to pick up the pieces when he gets ill again. I don't know whether it's worse when he's up or down—when he's down he takes to his bed, and when he's up he bosses everyone around and says the most horrible things.'

Cathy hadn't mentioned her mother, Mallory noticed. 'Does he live on his own?' Mallory asked.

Cathy shook her head. 'Mum left him years ago, when I was still in my teens. She couldn't cope with his illness. And a couple of years back he got so bad that I worried about him all the time, thinking he might have done something stupid and it'd be too late to help. So he moved in with us. Except...' She choked back a sob.

'It's very wearing,' Mallory said softly, 'living with someone who has manic depression. It's a very selfish illness. Your dad can't help it and he doesn't mean to worry you, but you're still in a difficult situation.'

'My husband says he does it for attention. Whenever we plan to do anything as a couple, Dad's suddenly ill so we can't do it. Mick says he does it on purpose—he stops taking his tablets so he's ill and we all have to fuss round him. Mick says if I don't do something, we'll end up losing the kids because the welfare people will say they're in unfit circumstances. That, or they'll leave home the minute they're sixteen and we'll never see them again. Eddie's at that difficult stage as it is. All I seem to get is slammed doors and sulks and...' She closed her eyes.

'What support are you getting?' Mallory asked. 'Does your father go to a day centre at all?'

'He won't go. Says he doesn't want to be with a bunch of loonies.'

'He'd probably be in for a pleasant surprise. It'd be a chance for him to meet new friends, learn some new interests. And he might get some counselling and advice there, too.'

Cathy spread her hands in desperation. 'I've *tried* to tell him. Dr Will's spent goodness knows how much time explaining to him—he's even dropped in at weekends to have a chat with him. But Dad won't have it. He won't even talk to the social worker or the woman from his mental health care team. He just turns his back on them until they leave. It doesn't help that every time he sees someone different. I know, I know, the team's overstretched and they can't promise to send the same person every time, but he's an old man. He can't cope with change. He'll talk to someone he knows, but making him tell the same story over and over again to people he'll never see again…it's pointless.'

'Have you thought about respite care—just to give you a couple of days' breathing space?'

Cathy shook her head. 'He won't go. Last time we tried it, so Mick and I could go away for a couple of days—it was our fifteenth wedding anniversary—he refused to speak or eat or drink and then he collapsed. He ended up in hospital and they rang us on Mick's mobile phone to tell us they'd taken him in.' Cathy bit her lip. 'I felt so guilty, we came home early. I don't think Mick's going to put up with it for much longer. But what can I do? I can't just abandon my dad and dump him in a home. It—it wouldn't be right. But I don't want this to break up my marriage either.'

'I don't think you've got manic depression,' Mallory said gently. 'I think you're under an awful lot of strain and feeling exactly the same as anyone else would in your situation. Perhaps if you could get your dad in to talk to me, maybe I can convince him that a day centre will really help him. If he went for two or three sessions a week, that'd give you and Mick some respite at the same time.'

'You really think he'd listen to you?' Cathy asked.

'I can try. And if he doesn't listen to me, there are some other people who could help.' Mallory smiled at Cathy.

'Hang on in there. There's a light at the end of the tunnel. Get him here to see me, and I'll do the rest.'

'And if he won't come?'

'Then I'll come and see him,' Mallory promised.

'Thanks, Dr Ryman. When I heard I was going to see the locum, I wasn't sure if you'd help me. Not the way Dr Will does—he listens and thinks and then helps.' She bit her lip. 'I just wish he'd be a bit more smiley. Back to the way he used to be when my kids were little, before the accident…'

Accident? But it had only happened a few days before. Or was Cathy talking about *another* accident, the one Hayley had mentioned?

But before Mallory could ask her what she meant, Cathy was already by the door. 'Thanks again, Dr Ryman.'

Mallory's next patient was equally worrying. 'So, how are you, Laura?' Mallory asked.

'OK.'

The brightness in the girl's voice didn't match her eyes; Mallory was immediately on guard. 'When was your last epileptic attack?' she asked casually.

'Can't remember. Ages ago. A few months.'

Mallory glanced at the screen. 'Any side effects from the tablets? Any drowsiness, dizziness, headaches?' She could see for herself that Laura didn't have a problem with acne or excess hair on her face. And the girl didn't look as if she was putting on weight, the other common side effect of the anti-epileptic drugs Laura was taking.

'I'm fine.'

No, you're not, Mallory thought. 'Then I'll be happy to give you a repeat prescription.' She tapped it into the computer. 'So tell me, Laura, are you learning to drive yet, or have you got a while to wait before you've had a whole year without a seizure?'

Laura suddenly crumpled. 'What's the point of learning

to drive?' she asked. 'I'm never going to be able to do anything. The epilepsy's always going to be in the way.'

'You're on medication. Provided you take it sensibly, it should keep your symptoms under control. There's no reason why you can't live a normal life.'

'But I'm epileptic. I could have a fit at any time. Supposing I'm out on the fells, leading a group, and I have a fit? Or I'm white-water rafting? I'm a danger to myself and the whole group.' She bit her lip. 'I'm no use to Mum and Dad.'

'Why not?'

'Because I'll never get a qualification as a leader. I can't do anything at Darrowthwaite Adventure Centre. And I can't go out with the mountain rescue team.'

'It's illegal to discriminate against you because of your epilepsy, unless there's an extremely good reason,' Mallory said. 'But there's no reason why you can't be on the mountain rescue's support team, manning the communications side. Communications are important—without them, the rescue team's working completely in the dark. And the same goes for the adventure centre. Leading a group isn't the only job you can do there.'

'But if I'm stuck behind a desk… Dad's already disappointed in me. I don't think he even sees me any more,' Laura said. 'I think that's why he let me stay on at school to do my A levels instead of letting me join the centre full time. It's all right for Sara—she's younger than me and she can do *everything*. Dad's already planning for when she leaves school and joins the centre full time. But me…I'm useless.'

'First of all,' Mallory said slowly, 'you can't live your life to please someone else.' She'd already learned that the hard way. 'And if your dad loves you as much as you love him, he'll understand that you can make just as much of a contribution to the centre on your own terms.'

'That's the point. I don't think he *does* love me. Because I'm useless.'

'No, you're not.' Mallory paused. 'What A levels are you doing?'

'Maths, art and computing.'

Mallory smiled. 'Then I think I know something that could be right up your street. And something that'll impress your dad. Do you have any free study periods?'

'This afternoon. It's a double free.'

'I'm free as well.' Mallory looked at the girl. 'How about we have a careers talk this afternoon? On the fells.'

'On the fells?'

'Uh-huh. I love walking but I'm a stranger round here—I bet you know the place like the back of your hand.'

'But…what if I have a fit?'

'I'm a qualified doctor. And we'll take my mobile phone in case I need extra help. Though I don't think we will.'

'Well…'

'I'll talk to your mum, clear it with her first. And then we'll go for a walk and talk through your options.'

'You'd really do that for me?'

Mallory nodded.

For the first time, Laura's smile was genuine. 'Thanks. What time?'

'Surgery finishes at twelve. I've got some paperwork to do first—but my boots are in my car. I'll meet you at the centre at, say, one?'

'All right. And thank you, Dr Ryman.'

Mallory didn't come home for lunch. The afternoon ticked away, slower and slower, and when the light faded Will started to get a bit concerned. Had Mallory gone out on the fells, slipped and fallen somewhere? Was she lost? Hurt? Hurt badly? But he had no idea where she'd gone.

She wouldn't have gone climbing without telling someone where she was going…would she? He knew she went climbing to think. And what they'd done this morning… Hell. His behaviour had driven her to climb. If anything happened to her, it would be his fault—just as it had been his fault that Roly had died.

When he saw headlights in his driveway and heard the crunch of footsteps on gravel a few moments later, he realised how tense his body had become—because he almost sagged in relief. And then he was furious.

'Where the hell have you been?'

Mallory dropped her doctor's bag on the floor and folded her arms. 'Good evening to you, too, Will.'

'I…' His voice faded. He was behaving like a spoilt child. And she didn't have to ask his permission to do anything. She was his locum, nothing more. 'Sorry. It was just… I was worried about you,' he admitted.

'I'm sorry—I'm supposed to be looking after you. I should have told you where I was going. I didn't realise how late it had got.' She sighed. 'I just went for a walk. With one of my patients, actually.'

His lips tightened. 'You might be a locum, but you're still bound by the same rules as any other doctor. You don't go out with your patients.'

'If it wasn't for the fact that you're on crutches and can't defend yourself, I'd slap your face for that. Number one,' she said crisply, 'I'm well aware of the rules. Number two, it's none of your business who I go out with. And, not that I'm under any obligation whatsoever to tell you this, I was with Laura Mercer.'

'Oh.'

'Oh,' she mimicked nastily. 'She's on your list so I'm not breaking patient confidentiality by telling you that she's epileptic. She came in for a repeat prescription and a check-up, and I wasn't happy about her. You know that epilepsy can be made worse by stress—well, she's stressed big time.

I got her to talk to me about it. She wants to leave school next year and join her family's business—but she doesn't think there's any point, not when she's epileptic. She doesn't think she'll be able to get a leader's qualification—even though she's on medication to control her condition, her health will affect her suitability. And even if she does get her qualification, supposing she has a fit when she's in the fells somewhere with a team, or she's white-water rafting or abseiling? It would put the whole team in danger, and it wouldn't exactly be a good ad for her parents' business. Plus, she feels her dad doesn't love her any more because of her disability. The kid needed someone to talk to.' Mallory spread her hands. 'So we went for a walk this afternoon. We had a chat. And I think we've got a solution to her problem.'

'Right.'

'Right.' She lifted her chin.

Will knew what she expected. 'OK. I'm sorry.'

'Sorry?' she prompted.

'For going off at the deep end.'

'And are you going to tell me why?'

'I don't know what you mean.'

'Come on, Will. There's something going on here I don't know about. I've already worked out it's something to do with climbing and something to do with your girlfriend, wife, whoever. A woman, anyway.'

'You're jumping to conclusions.'

'No, I'm trying to stop myself putting my foot in it.'

He scowled. 'It's nothing to do with you.'

'Oh, yes, it is. I'm your locum. And I'm supposed to be helping to look after you. If something's upsetting you, it's likely to affect how well you heal. So talk.'

'There's nothing to talk about.'

'There are two ways we can do this,' Mallory said. 'The

civilised way, over coffee—the way I told you about what happened with Lindy. Or the tough way.'

He glowered but didn't rise to the bait.

She gave him a saccharine-sweet smile. 'Marion tells me you're bored. You've phoned the surgery half a dozen times today on the off-chance there might be an excuse for you to come in.'

'I'm not used to sitting around doing nothing. It doesn't suit me.'

'You're not "doing nothing". You're letting your body heal.' She paused. 'Imagine what it'd be like if you didn't have your crutches so you couldn't have a change of scene. All your books and magazines were out of reach. Ditto the remote control for your stereo. So you were stuck in a chair, bored stiff, and there was nothing you could do about it.'

'Are you threatening me, Mallory Ryman?'

'What do you think?'

He stared at her. She lifted her chin and met his gaze unflinchingly.

Obviously she wasn't going to give a millimetre. Will didn't want to tell her the truth about what had happened with Roly and Julie. But even worse was the prospect of being stuck here, with nothing to take his mind off his thoughts. Nothing to take his mind off his memories.

So he had no choice. He had to tell her. *Some* of it, anyway.

CHAPTER SEVEN

'IT'S not pretty,' Will said. 'And I'll understand if you want to move on.'

'You're not making any sense at all,' Mallory told him baldly. 'Look, I know there was an accident—an accident *before* this one. And that picture of you with…' she gestured to the photograph '…your brother, I presume, is obviously at the top of a climb somewhere. You bit my head off when I asked you about your girlfriend. So she died in a climbing accident, right?'

'No. Julie's still alive. She's working for Médicins Sans Frontières.'

So what was the problem? 'In the hospital,' she said quietly, 'you made me talk to you. You listened. I nearly killed one of my patients. Whatever you did, it can't be as bad as that.'

'Oh, but it can,' Will said bitterly. 'My brother died— and it was all my fault.'

It was the last thing she'd expected to hear. Will had been responsible for his brother's death. *That* must have been the accident people had alluded to. And as for his girlfriend…maybe he'd felt so guilty that he'd pushed her away. The same way he was trying to push her away. Yes, that all made sense.

She took a deep breath. 'Will, you made me face my demons. It's time to face yours. But I'm going to make some coffee first. Want some?'

He didn't answer.

'I'm not going to let you retreat into silence so don't

even try it. You made me talk to you about Lindy. Now it's my turn to listen—and your turn to talk.'

She might be small and slender, but Mallory was incredibly determined, Will thought as he watched her leave the room. And she was a climber. He knew her type: she'd tackle any mountain. Just as he once had.

Except this particular mountain was too big to conquer.

Mallory returned and handed him a mug of coffee—hot, strong and dark, just as he liked it—and an opened packet of pecan shortbread. 'Right. Tell me about your brother. The one in the photo with you?' She gestured to the picture.

He nodded. 'That's Roly.'

'Older than you?'

'Fifteen minutes younger.'

'Your twin.' She looked thoughtful.

Will sighed. 'He was a doctor, too. In A and E.' He shrugged. 'Roly couldn't have done anything else really. The pace in A and E suited him to a T. He liked living on the edge. That's why he climbed. He said that when you sat on the roof of the world, everything was so much clearer.'

Mallory nodded. 'It is. And you should know—you used to climb, too, didn't you?'

'Yes.'

'And?'

His lip curled. 'Lost my nerve.'

'Will, accidents happen. You know the risks before you climb. And you don't strike me as the reckless sort who can't be bothered to check their equipment or that any holds are secure before you use them.' Her eyes were very blue, very piercing. 'Or were you, before the accident?'

'No.' He closed his eyes. That had been Roly, not him.

'So it wasn't your fault, then.'

'Yes, it was.'

'I don't see how. Explain.'

His jaw set. 'It won't change what happened.'

'And I can't change what happened with Lindy, but you made me tell you about it. Fair's fair—it's your turn.'

Will sighed and opened his eyes again. 'OK. Roly and I… It's a weird thing, being a twin. You're either so close you're joined at the hip or…it's as if you're fighting for your own identity the whole time, and the person you fight most is your twin.'

'And you and Roly fought?'

He nodded. 'I don't know if it would have been better if we'd been identical twins. But it was like a competition between us most of the time. Who'd get the best exam marks. Who'd be picked to play for the school team. Who'd come first in any kind of race. It got worse when we were teenagers. Because he was the younger, he felt he had to outdo me in everything. And when I got into climbing, he had to do it too, and do it better.' Will bit his lip. 'At first I think he did it because of me. And then he grew to love climbing itself. The challenge of getting to the top. The way it makes you feel alive, remember you're human—it's not safe and cocooned, like the everyday world you live in.'

'And you miss it,' Mallory said softly.

Will ignored the question. 'Roly always took more risks than I did. He'd always take the most difficult route up to the top, he'd always climb freestyle rather than belaying, whereas I always played it safe, made sure I didn't get into difficulties or drag anyone else into a mess.'

'So you're a team player and he wasn't.' Mallory shrugged. 'No big deal.'

'It wasn't a good twin, bad twin thing,' Will protested. 'Roly was fun to be with. But he had a reckless streak, and girls just loved it. Too much, perhaps—he partied with the best of them at uni. And he flunked his first-year exams.'

'And you came top of the year?' Mallory guessed.

'How I did isn't important. But they were going to throw him out. I talked them into giving him another chance—not that he ever knew that. It would have killed him to know he had me to thank.'

'So you didn't actually like each other?'

Will sighed. 'It's complicated. A twin thing. You love each other and hate each other at the same time. The fact he had to repeat the year did us both a favour—it took all the competition away and freed us both to do what we really wanted to do. I think we got on a lot better after that. Maybe we should have gone to separate universities in the first place.' He drummed his fingers on the table. 'I decided to come back home to Cumbria and be a GP—I'm happier in the country than the city, and I wanted to do something that was part of the community, follow my patients through. Roly finished his rotations in London and then took off for the States, specialised in trauma medicine. Though funnily enough we both did the same kind of thing in our spare time. We both joined the local mountain rescue team. So when he came back here to take up a senior post in A and E at the local hospital, I offered him my spare room until he'd found his own place.'

'And?'

Oh, God. He really *couldn't* tell her the whole story. 'I thought we'd both grown out of the competition thing. I thought he'd grown up and we could maybe be friends.' He shrugged. 'Roly joined the mountain rescue team here. And he was called out one night. The rope snapped, and he went straight down the cliff. There was nothing anyone could do. He died. And it was all my fault.'

'No.' Mallory took the mug from Will's hand, then wrapped her fingers round his. 'Will, if you join a rescue team, you know you can be called out at any time. It's part of the deal. The accident was…well, it was just that. An *accident*. Horrible, because you lost your brother, but it wasn't your fault.'

'It was,' Will insisted. 'It should have been me.'

'No. It was just the luck of the draw. They called him.'

'You don't understand.' He extricated his fingers from hers. 'It should have been me. Except they couldn't reach me because I'd turned my phone off.'

'We all need five minutes' peace sometimes. Don't beat yourself up about it.'

'I was being self-indulgent.'

'Right. Says the GP who does home visits when they're not scheduled—and in his own free time, come to that. The GP who says patients can call him at any time for a chat, and means it. The GP who doesn't even take his days off. And no, I'm not telling you which of your patients grassed on you,' Mallory said. 'But if you've been driving yourself at this pace since the accident—which was when?'

'Five years ago.'

'If you've been driving yourself this hard for five years,' she said, 'I'm surprised you haven't given yourself high blood pressure or even a heart attack. Don't you think you've more than paid for your five-minute break?'

'It wasn't five minutes.'

'Ten, then. Whatever.'

He shook his head. 'Even if my phone *had* been on, I wouldn't have been able to go out. I was drunk.'

She rolled her eyes. 'For goodness' sake, Will. We all did it as students—and most of us do it once in a while. When you're having a good time over dinner with friends and don't realise how many times you've topped up your glass until you walk outside and it hits you. You're a GP, Will. That doesn't stop you being human.'

He was a GP. So he should have known better. A lot better. 'I was *deliberately* drunk,' he said through gritted teeth.

And then wished he hadn't.

Because Mallory took his hand again. Held it. Just as she would a patient's, letting him know that she was there and it was safe to talk to her. 'So now we come to the real problem,' she said softly. 'What *really* happened, Will?'

'I don't want to talk about it.'

'OK.' She released his hand. 'Now, crutches, remote control, books—'

'You wouldn't.'

'Try me.'

He shook his head in despair. 'Mallory, I...'

'Hey.' She curled her fingers back round his. 'If one of your patients was feeling bad about something that happened years ago, driving himself into the ground because of it, you'd get him to tell you what the real problem was, yes?'

'Yes.'

'And he'd know that he could tell you anything because you were his doctor and whatever he said was confidential.'

'You're not my doctor,' Will pointed out.

'But I'm *a* doctor. Bound by the same oath. I'm not going to judge you, Will, but whatever you're holding on to is corroding you from within. If you don't let it out, soon there won't be any Will Cooper left.'

He was silent.

'And that matters, Will,' she said softly. 'It really matters. Tell me.'

'Nobody knows about this.' Nobody except him, Roly and Julie. Roly was dead and Julie was thousands of miles away.

'All the more reason for you to tell me.'

He said nothing for a long, long time. But Mallory was an experienced GP—she was good at the waiting game. At last he sighed. 'When Roly was away, I met someone on the MR team. Julie. I fell head over heels in love with her.

She was all I ever thought I wanted in a woman—she was clever, funny, beautiful, brave. She was a nurse practitioner on the surgical ward at the local hospital. She liked all the same things I did, loved climbing… She was my soulmate. And she loved me, too. We'd even set a date for the wedding.' His face darkened. 'Then Roly came home. And it was love at first sight.'

Her eyes widened. 'You mean they had an affair?'

'They swore not. They said they'd never betray me like that—that they'd told me before things had gone too far between them.'

'But you don't believe it?'

Will sighed. 'I don't know. I don't know what to think. I've sat at Roly's grave and asked him heaven knows how many times.' Not just about whether they had an affair. Whether Roland really *had* loved Julie, and if it had been more than just taking something his brother had had and he'd wanted. 'But he can't tell me now—can he?'

'What about Julie?' she asked softly.

'I can't… I'd like to think she was telling me the truth. But I know Roly of old. The Pied Piper had nothing on Roly—Roly could charm everyone. Even our mother. You'd think as a JP she'd know when someone was conning her. But Roly could do it every time.' He swallowed hard. 'The night they told me about it, Roly moved out. Julie moved out with him. And I…' He laughed mirthlessly. 'I wasn't on call that night and it was my weekend off. So I decided to get drunk, *really* drunk, in an attempt to blot out the pain. I've never been a whisky drinker— that was Roly—and I've never touched the stuff since, but that night I turned my mobile phone off, took my landline off the hook, turned the stereo up loud and drank my way through half a bottle of whisky. If I hadn't been so bloody spineless, just thinking about poor little me, I'd have taken that phone call. And I'd have been sober enough to make a difference.'

'Oh, come on, Will. Your brother went off with your fiancée. It must have been a hell of a shock. Just about anyone in your situation would have got roaring drunk. You wouldn't have been human if you'd just calmly carried on as if nothing had happened.'

Will ignored her.

'So why did you stop climbing?' Her eyes narrowed. 'You *didn't* lose your nerve, did you?'

'I just can't do it any more. Every time I even look at a mountain, I think about Roly and how much he loved climbing. And how he died. And it shouldn't have happened.'

'It was an accident, Will. A tragic accident.' She squeezed his hand. 'So, if you hate mountains so much, how come you're still working in Darrowthwaite, right in the middle of climbing territory?'

'I'd already let the MR team down. I couldn't let the town down as well by running away. I'm their GP. They need me.'

She rubbed her thumb across his knuckles, still holding his fingers tightly. 'Remember what you told me? Everyone deserves a second chance—don't be so hard on yourself. Don't you think that applies to you, too?'

'I can't climb any more. I just freeze. So I'd be a liability to the team,' he told her.

'What about the dog?'

'Huh?' He stared at her, surprised.

'You have precisely three photographs on display. One of you with Roly, one of a couple I assume are your parents, and one of a dog. A Border collie.'

'A red merle,' Will enlightened her.

'Did Julie take him with her?'

'Rusty wasn't Julie's dog. He was mine. And he's living with someone else now. He's a trained SARDA dog.'

Search And Rescue Dog Association. She suddenly remembered their conversation at Furze End Farm. 'The Johnsons. Is he their dogs' brother?'

'Yeah.'

'Oh, Will. Couldn't you have kept him?'

'No. I told you, I trained him as a rescue dog. That's what he does.' And, wrench as it had been to give up his dog, Will had known that he had to do the right thing. To make up in part for doing the wrong thing that terrible night.

'Does it ever strike you that you're wallowing?'

He stared at her in shock. Those were the last words he'd expected to hear. He'd just bared his soul to her—and she was accusing him of wallowing?

'Think about it,' she said. 'Your brother died *in an accident*. And what's your response? You give up climbing, you give up your dog. Maybe someone should have bought you a hair shirt to go with it.'

'Mallory, you—'

She refused to let him interrupt. 'You're an experienced climber. A trained doctor. You could be saving lives out there, Will.'

'I've already told you, I can't climb any more.'

'Not with your leg in pins and your arm in plaster, I grant you. But there's no reason why you can't climb again when you've healed. You say you were selfish that night in getting drunk—how much more selfish is it to deny people your skill?'

Will stared at her, hurt and angry, clenching his good fist.

'Will refusing to climb any more bring Roly back?' She answered her own question. 'No, it won't.'

'That's outrageous,' he said between clenched teeth.

'No, Will, it's the truth. Yes, it was horrible that Roly decided to go off with your fiancée. Yes, it's sad that he was killed. But it's about time you got over it and stopped burying your head in the sand. Stopped burying yourself in work. Started living life to the full again.'

'I don't believe I'm hearing this.'

'What next? Are you going to ask me to leave so you can have another locum, one who'll just leave you to fester in your own little world of misery?'

'Just where do you get off, telling me what to do?'

'You've been feeling sorry for yourself for five years, from the sound of things.'

'Says the woman who resigned after she made just one mistake.'

'But at least I'm trying to sort it out. Unlike you.'

Will was about to get to his feet and storm out when he remembered that he couldn't. Instead, he glowered at Mallory. 'I think you'd better find somewhere else to stay.'

'Fine.' She stood up, put her hands on her hips and glared back. 'But, speaking as a GP, I can't allow you to stay here on your own. Whatever you think, you're really not fit enough to manage alone. Shall I ring a convalescent home or your mother?'

'You really know how to hit below the belt, don't you?'

'I have two older brothers. Mikey and Jonno made damned sure I wasn't going to be a spoiled brat.'

'And what do they think of your going off to sulk up a mountain?'

'About the same as I think of your *not* going back up a mountain.' She lifted her chin. 'It's self-indulgent in the extreme.'

Her candour disarmed him and he smiled. 'So you're preaching what you don't practise?' He flapped his unin- jured hand at her. 'Oh, sit down, Mallory. I'm not going to chuck you out of job or home. It wouldn't help either of us and it won't change the past.'

Mallory had thought the full smile would be something else. But this…was unexpected. Because it made her heart flip and her pulse race. Smiling, Will Cooper was a lot more dangerous than he was when he was scowling.

She sat down. Not because he'd told her to—because her knees were feeling that tiniest bit weak.

'All right. So you've bearded the lion in his den.'

'Set one foot in the den, more like. When are you going to admit that you're being selfish?'

'Back off, Mallory.' His eyes glinted a warning at her.

'For now. But don't think I'm going to let it rest.'

'Very brave. But, of course, you have two brothers. You know how to nag to get your own way.' He gave her a speculative look. 'Exactly how brave are you feeling?'

'Why?'

'Because I think we have something else to talk about.'

'Something else?'

'Mmm.' Will couldn't help it. The memory of that morning's kiss made him lick his lower lip to see if he could still taste her.

She flushed instantly. 'Y-you mean Craig Clarke's tests?' she asked, her tone falsely bright. 'They came back today, actually. Positive serum precipitins. So I'm fairly sure we're talking about EAA. I've referred him for a chest X-ray—we should have the results back next week, and I think we'll see the classic honeycomb shadowing and mottling. Let's just hope we've caught him early enough, before his lungs start to fibrose.'

'I didn't mean Craig's tests.'

'Then what did you want to talk about?' she asked.

'This morning.'

'There's nothing to say,' she lied.

He gave her a look that said he didn't buy it. Not at all.

'I've been walking in the fells and I'm starving so I'm hogging the bathroom, as of now. Perhaps you could order dinner while I have a bath?' she suggested.

That flush was interesting. As was the way her pupils had expanded. So she was rattled, was she? That made two of them. And right now he had no idea what he was going to do about it. What either of them was going to do about it.

CHAPTER EIGHT

MALLORY was edgy around Will for the rest of the evening, so there was only one thing he could do. Back off before he scared her away for good. It seemed to work, because she relaxed with him again. And, to his relief, she didn't mention the Roly situation. It was as if she was giving him a chance to think about what she'd said and make up his own mind about it.

Was he really being selfish? He'd thought he'd done the right thing, leaving the team—making sure he didn't let anyone down again. And he'd given Rusty to one of the other trainers because it had been the right thing to do. It would have been greedy to keep the dog as just a pet when he'd been trained to help people who needed him.

But that wasn't the way Mallory saw it. At all. In fact, she thought the opposite. So who was right?

He thought about it for days and he still couldn't come up with the answer.

'Your week's trial is up,' he said on the Friday night. 'So what's the verdict?'

'It's a two-way thing,' she said. 'You go first.'

Will nodded. 'From my point of view, it works. You get on well with the rest of the team. The patients like you—and, even better, you've managed to get through to some really difficult cases, persuade them to try something different.' He looked at her. 'Some of them have even told Marion they hope you'll stay. So will you?'

'If you think I'm up to the job.'

'I do,' he said honestly. 'I've sat in with you in surgery

and house calls, and you've done everything I would have done in those situations. And I can speak as a patient as well. You've kept a check on my leg and made sure there aren't any signs of infection. You've kept an eye on my pain relief without making me feel like a helpless child. You've made little changes here and there to make my life easier and give me some of my independence back—I can even take a shower on my own.'

He wished he hadn't said that. Because he had an immediate vision of taking a shower with Mallory. A vision that left him extremely shaky.

And he'd felt the tiniest tremor in her fingertips on the second and third times she'd shaved him. A tremor that had been matched by a sudden surge in his pulse. Not that he'd worked out what he could do about it. Right now, he couldn't even walk properly, let alone do what he *really* wanted to do with Mallory Ryman.

He forced himself to clear his mind. 'So—are you staying?'

She nodded. 'Yes. I like the practice and I like the people around here. And—' her gaze was definitely challenging '—the climbing.'

'That's twenty pence you owe the cake fund.'

'I bought a round of cakes today.'

'Then call it the first instalment for next week's.'

'You're all in this together,' she said, mock-complaining. 'Well, make it forty pence. I'm going climbing tomorrow. And, before you start fussing, I'm not going on my own. I'm going with Laura Mercer.'

'Supposing she has a fit?'

'Then she'll have a doctor on hand,' Mallory said lightly, though he could sense the edge of disapproval in her voice.

'I wasn't trying to put her down,' he said, guessing what the problem was.

'Good. She can do enough of that on her own—and so can her father.'

'What is it with you and fathers?' Will asked.

'I don't know what you mean.' Her voice was clipped.

He'd clearly hit a raw nerve. 'Your father doesn't like you climbing, does he?'

'My father just needs to learn that you can't live your life to please someone else.'

There was more to it than just her climbing, Will thought. But what? Was it her career? Or something else?

But she obviously wasn't going to tell him. She simply used her usual excuse—that she wanted a bath before dinner.

Mallory was gone before Will got up in the morning. She'd left him a note to say that Debbie, his next-door neighbour, would be in a couple of times during the day to check if he needed anything. Mallory wasn't sure what time she'd be back, but she'd be checking in regularly with the Mercers, and her mobile phone would stay switched on if he needed her.

The cottage seemed empty without her. Way too big. During the week it was bearable, because he knew she was only at the surgery or on house calls, and she'd be back soon...

Will gave a yelp as he burned his mouth on his coffee— Mallory had left him a pump-action Thermos that he could use one-handed. No. He didn't feel like that about Mallory. He *couldn't*. He wasn't ever going to fall in love again, remember? Not like he had with Julie.

So when Debbie rapped on the door and walked into the kitchen, Will was more charming than he'd intended to be. Because Debbie was just the sort of woman he ought to fall in love with. Sweet and domesticated. The type who made her own cakes and would fuss around him. The sort who wouldn't nag him to go climbing again.

'I was wondering if you'd like a change of scenery—I mean, it must be so frustrating, being stuck indoors,' Debbie said.

'It is, a bit,' Will agreed.

'Perhaps, um, you'd like to go out for a drink with me tonight?'

'I'd love to,' Will said. 'In fact, why don't we make it dinner?'

Debbie flushed prettily. 'That'd be nice. Thank you.'

'Perfect,' Mallory said as they reached the summit of Blencathra and sat down on a rock. 'I really needed this.'

'Me, too,' Laura said. 'It's the first time I've climbed for ages, without worrying that it was all going to go wrong and I'd be a burden on everyone else.'

'Good. So now you know you can still do it.' All she had to do now was get Will to realise that, too. Mallory smiled. 'What does your dad think about the web site design idea?'

'Cool.' Laura beamed. 'I did a couple of roughs for him. And he liked them. He said he'd never realised how clever I was.'

Her father's approval was clearly the thing Laura most wanted in the world, Mallory thought. She'd been there herself. And failed. Spectacularly. Dominic Ryman had never actually told her he disapproved of her, but she knew. She'd seen it in his eyes the day she'd told him she wasn't going to marry Geoff. The day she'd told him she'd resigned from Charles's practice. The day she'd told him she wasn't sure if she still wanted to be a doctor.

'Funny, we've lived next door to each other for over a year—but I feel we hardly know each other,' Debbie said.

'We both work, we're both busy at weekends,' Will said.

'Even so. I should have thought to ask you round for a barbecue or something—I normally have one every summer for my colleagues.'

'I'm on call a lot.' He paused. 'It's really kind of you to have checked up on me. Interrupting your weekend.'

'No problem. I wasn't doing anything special anyway.'

She had such a sweet smile. She was nice—really and genuinely nice. So why was he sitting here, wishing that it was someone else opposite him? Wishing that a certain auburn-haired woman with beautiful cheekbones and stunning eyes and...

'You look a million miles away,' Debbie said.

'Just tired,' Will lied, not wanting to hurt her.

'Sorry. I should have thought. The accident must have really knocked it out of you. And you're still on crutches.'

'Not your fault. Doctors are the worst patients—we never take our own advice,' Will said lightly, though he felt like a heel. How could he do this—go out with one woman, when another one was in his head the whole time?

'Maybe we ought to go.'

He shook his head. 'We've ordered pudding.'

'I don't mind.'

He did. It wasn't fair of him to lead Debbie on, let her think that this could become something more. He had to stop this right now. 'Debbie, I'm glad we came out tonight.'

'Really?' She brightened.

'Because it's made me realise what a good friend I have next door,' he continued gently.

'Oh. Yes.'

That flush again. As if she'd thought he'd meant something else—and was trying to cover up her disappointment. 'The thing is...I'm not looking for a relationship.'

'No, of course not. You and Mallory—'

Will shook his head. 'There isn't a me and Mallory.

She's my locum,' he said. 'And she's staying with me because that was the only way the hospital would let me out. I was engaged a while back. It didn't work out—but I don't think I'm really ready to move on.' It wasn't quite an untruth.

'I see.'

'But I could use a friend,' he said. 'So maybe we could do this again some time—as friends?'

'Of course. That'd be nice.'

But Debbie didn't say much else over pudding or coffee. And Will felt worse and worse with every passing minute. His judgement was definitely in lousy mode. And he wasn't sure how to make things right.

Gone out for dinner with Debbie. See you later. W.

Well, it was what she'd been angling for, wasn't it? Mallory thought as she glared at Will's note. She'd pushed them together, asking Debbie to check on him while she was out climbing. The local primary school teacher and the local doctor. It was the perfect match, wasn't it? Debbie was just the kind of sweet, domesticated woman Will probably wanted. The kind Will *needed*.

Out to dinner. He hadn't said where. Maybe at Debbie's cottage next door? Debbie was probably cooking for him even now…

No. Mallory gritted her teeth. She was *not* jealous.

But somehow the glow she normally felt after a climb had faded. Even a hot shower with plenty of lime and tea tree oil shower gel failed to restore her equanimity. Which slipped even more when she contemplated her evening meal. She'd refused the Mercers' invitation to stay for dinner, saying that she'd better get back to check on Will. Even though she knew he was being looked after perfectly well.

More than perfectly well if he'd gone out to dinner with Debbie.

She scowled. She was starving, but at this time on a Saturday evening she'd have to wait ages for a take-away and even longer for a table if she went out for a meal. Not that she fancied that idea anyway—she might end up in the same place as Will and Debbie, if they hadn't gone next door. Come to think of it, Debbie's lights hadn't been on…

Cross with herself for speculating—she was *not* interested in Dr Will Cooper, she reminded herself—she nipped out to the local supermarket and bought herself some spinach, Roquefort, bacon and a pack of English muffins. She'd just assembled her meal and put it under the grill when Will manoeuvred himself into the kitchen.

'What's this?' He pantomimed shock. 'Should someone be taking a photograph?'

'Ha, ha.'

'Mallory Ryman, cooking. Well, well, well. Going in for being a domestic goddess, are we?'

'Shut up, Will. This isn't proper cooking. I've been climbing—' she threw the word at him like a weapon '—I'm hungry and I'd like to eat in peace.'

Will stooped down to look under the grill. 'Not proper cooking, hmm? And that is…?'

'Glorified cheese on toast.'

'Wrong shape. Wrong colour.'

She rolled her eyes. 'Don't make a big thing about it. The principle's the same—you can use toast, bagels, crumpets, whatever. It's just toasted English muffins, topped with a couple of things and then some cheese.'

'"Some cheese". Hardly the way to describe Roquefort,' Will said, eyeing the packet.

'Aren't you supposed to be out with Debbie?' she demanded.

'Uh-huh.'

'So where is she?'

'She had some marking to do.'

'On Saturday night?'

'Reports for a parents' evening this week,' Will said.

He sounded casual enough. Her matchmaking between him and Debbie clearly hadn't been that successful. And he wasn't that upset about it.

And she certainly shouldn't be feeling so relieved about it.

'Are you having a glass of wine with that?' he asked.

'Yes. And you're on painkillers, so you can't.'

'Red wine,' he remarked in disgust as he saw the opened bottle standing on the worktop. 'The woman's drinking red wine.' He heaved himself over to the worktop and inspected the label. 'Decent red wine. And eating Roquefort. And she expects me to sit and watch her.'

'You don't have to sit in here.'

'My leg hurts.'

'Then take your analgesics. Look, leave me alone or I'll burn this,' she snapped.

'Whoo! Temper,' he taunted.

'All right, you can have a glass of wine,' she said through gritted teeth. 'But if it makes you feel rough, it's your own fault.'

'Thank you.' He leaned against the worktop, reached up into a cupboard and took down two glasses. 'I'm glad you've uncorked it already. I'd have had to ask for help, there.'

She ignored him and retrieved her muffins from the grill.

'Looks nice,' he offered as he filled both glasses. 'For someone who can't cook.'

'I didn't say I *couldn't* cook. I said I *didn't* cook,' Mallory corrected him, adding salad to her plate and drizzling balsamic vinegar over it before sprinkling shaved Parmesan over the top. 'Anything that takes more than ten minutes to prepare and cook is a waste of time in my book. Think of all the things you could be doing instead.'

'I take it your speciality's stir-fries?'

She stared suspiciously at him. 'Where's this leading?'

'Nowhere. No demands. Though I might bear it in mind next time you nag me about things that are absolutely nothing to do with you.' He sat down and lifted his glass in a toast to her. 'Cheers. Good climb?'

'Yes, thank you.'

'Is any of that cheese going spare?'

She rolled her eyes. 'I thought you went out for dinner?'

'I did. But I have this thing about cheese. And I love Roquefort. And cheese goes very well with wine.'

'Oh, for goodness' sake.' Mallory fetched Will a plate and a knife, and opened a packet of oatcakes for him. '*Now* can I eat my dinner in peace, or was there something else you wanted?'

A kiss. He almost said it aloud.

This was really, incredibly stupid. He had no intention of getting involved again. Not beyond friendship. Particularly with a woman who reminded him so much of his past, what he used to be. Yet Mallory Ryman sent him straight into a tailspin.

Hell. He'd even tried going out with the kind of woman he thought would be better for him. And it hadn't worked. Because he wanted…Mallory.

But he couldn't have her. He couldn't expect her to give up climbing for him, yet he couldn't face climbing again. Ever. And there was no middle road.

CHAPTER NINE

'WE WERE right about Mark Johnson,' Mallory said, a couple of days later. 'I had all his test results back today. His blood serum iron and ferritin levels are up, and the liver biopsy was pretty much what I'd expected. He's coming in for his first venesection tomorrow, and his son's coming in to give me a blood sample so I can screen him for the condition, too.'

'Good call,' Will said. 'Anything else I should know about?'

'Craig Clarke's chest X-rays. Good news—we caught him early and although there's a bit of mottling, we're not talking fibrosis. He's coming back in a couple of days so I can see how the steroids are working and if he needs a longer course. And he's promised not to play in the barn or anywhere else that's had hay stored in it and might contain moulds. Rita's going to warn his friends' parents, too, so he's not put in a situation where he's going to react badly.'

Will nodded. 'Prevention's the best thing.'

'I've sent Olivia Hart the information I promised—she's got an appointment with an acupuncturist in Keswick and she's seriously considering trying St John's wort. Cathy Becker still hasn't persuaded her dad to come in and talk to me, so I'm going to pop in and see him later in the week.'

'Good luck,' Will said feelingly. 'I'm still feeling guilty about him—I was the one who talked Cathy into sending him to respite care for the weekend. Mick's sister was going to look after the kids.'

'It's not your fault he ended up in hospital.'

'Some patients,' Will said softly, 'are hard to help.'

Yes. And Will himself was a case in point. 'But that doesn't mean you stop trying.'

'No. And you've already proved you're good at getting through to people.'

Mallory smiled back. Though she could have corrected him. *Some* people. She hadn't been able to get through to her father. Last time she'd phoned home, he'd still managed to work it into the conversation about how it wasn't too late to change her mind and all she had to do was call Geoff and make it up with him. In the end she'd found herself switching off, punctuating the conversation with 'Mmm' in what she hoped were the right places, until he'd given up and passed the phone to her mother.

'Are you all right?'

Will was too good at picking up her mood, she decided. 'Fine,' she said. 'Just feeling a bit…earthbound today.'

'The temperature hasn't gone above freezing all day,' Will said, nodding at the window. Thick frost was still visible on the window-sill.

'And that doesn't take the wind-chill factor into account,' Mallory said. 'I'm not stupid. I don't take unnecessary risks.'

'But you've got itchy feet.'

She shrugged. 'I'll live with it. Want a coffee?'

'Thanks.' It wasn't just the climbing that was upsetting her, Will was sure. But he wasn't going to press her any further. She'd tell him when the time was right.

A few days later, their truce about the climbing issue was forced off kilter. Mallory was browsing in a bookshop when she heard a distant beeping. It kept growing louder. When she realised it was her mobile phone, she took it from her handbag and peered at the display. It wasn't a number she knew. Probably a wrong number. She sighed and answered it anyway. 'Hello?'

'Mallory? Is that you?'

Mallory recognised the voice at the other end of the line. 'Laura? What's up?'

'I'm at Darrowthwaite Mountain Rescue Team Base. We've had a call in but I can't get hold of most of the team. Are you doing house calls or due in surgery?'

'No, I'm in the middle of Darrowthwaite. I was running a couple of errands for Will.'

'Sorry to ask, but I need one more person. Can you help us? It's an emergency,' Laura said. 'You said you've done mountain rescue work.'

'It was a while ago. And I haven't signed up with the Darrowthwaite team.'

'I know, I know, and you haven't done probation with them—but if your last team will vouch for you... Please, Mallory? It's Ian Cawsey—he's a diabetic. He's at Sharp Edge. His climbing partner says he's collapsed.'

Which could mean diabetic coma. Which could be very serious if left untreated, depending on whether his blood had too much or too little sugar. 'OK, I'm on my way to you now,' Mallory said. She gave Laura a number. 'Ask for Becky Hunter—she'll fax over a reference.'

'Thanks, Mallory.'

She cut the connection and rang Will on her way back to the cottage. Every minute counted and she didn't want to waste time in an argument. 'Will, it's me.'

Her tension must be audible, she thought, because he picked up on it straight away. 'What's up?'

'Laura rang me. It's her shift manning the base—and she can't get hold of most of the rescue team. There's been an accident. Possible diabetic coma. I'm a qualified climber and I'm a doctor.' She took a deep breath. 'Will, I know this is going to bring back bad memories for you and I'm sorry, but I've done mountain rescue work in the past and they need me to help.'

'Where?'

This was the worst bit. Telling him it was the same place where his brother had died. There was no way she could soften the blow. 'It's Sharp Edge, Will.'

'Usually is.'

His voice was clipped and she could just imagine what was going through his mind. 'They need me, Will,' she said softly. 'I'm on my way back to the cottage now. My doctor's bag is in your living room.'

'Have you got dextrose and glucagon?'

'I think so.'

'I'll check. If you haven't, I'll ring Marion and ask her to have some ready at the surgery reception.'

'Thanks. Better check for insulin, too, in case he's hyperglycaemic rather than hypoglycaemic.' If she got it the wrong way round and gave him insulin when his blood sugar was already too low, he could die.

'Who is it?'

'Ian Cawsey. Is he one of ours?'

'Yes. Type two diabetes, diagnosed a few months back. So it's probably a hypo.' There was a pause that seemed to last far longer than it actually did. 'Better take my car,' he said gruffly.

'Thanks, Will. I owe you one.'

'Ring me if you need me.'

Had she heard that right? Had he offered to help with the rescue, in the only way he *could* help, right now? Or maybe she'd imagined it. Maybe she'd hoped so much that this would make him rethink his involvement with the MR team that she'd heard what she'd wanted to hear rather than what he'd actually said.

She tried for levity. 'How about I do you a stir-fry when

I get home? Prawns in ginger. Takes four minutes so it's not cooking.'

'Yeah. I'll hold you to that.'

Ten minutes later, Mallory was on her way to Blencathra with Rob Viner, one of the senior members of the rescue team, Euan Patteson and Bryan Gould.

'Becky Hunter faxed over a reference for your time with their team. Laura's vouched for you,' Rob said, 'and we know you're standing in for Dr Cooper. He's vouched for you, too—as he used to be our main assessor, that's good enough for me.'

Will had assessed people wanting to join the mountain rescue team? This got worse and worse. Somehow she was going to have to get through to him, make him realise how much he was depriving the team. They needed him just as much as his patients did.

And this made it definite she shouldn't ring him on the pretence that she needed his help. He'd recognise the ruse for what it was and she'd push him further away. No, she needed to give him space to think about it. But not too much.

She looked at Rob. 'I know that under any other circumstances I wouldn't be allowed out until you'd given me a trial and I'd served a probationary period with your team. And I promise I won't let you down. What can you tell me about Ian Cawsey?'

'Fifty. Diabetic. Experienced climber—so's his climbing partner, Martin Evans.'

'He's recently diagnosed, isn't he, with type two diabetes?' Mallory asked.

'Fairly,' Euan said. 'He's on tablets, not injections.'

As Will had said, that made it more likely Ian Cawsey's blood sugar was too low rather than too high. Mallory rolled her eyes. 'Don't tell me—he didn't think to take glucose sweets with him or even a sugar lump.'

'Apparently he did,' Bryan explained, 'but when he slipped and fell earlier, he ripped his pocket and they went straight down the gully.'

'So what happened?' Mallory asked.

'Martin says that Ian was a bit clumsy and snappy with him, then he suddenly came over a bit dizzy. They stopped for a bit and the next thing Martin knew, Ian had passed out. Luckily they weren't in a dead area for mobile phones so he rang 999. He's going to call us if Ian gets any worse.'

'Right.' It was sounding more and more like low blood sugar—clumsiness and aggression were typical early warning symptoms. 'Where are they?'

'A hundred and fifty feet down the usual gully.' Rob's face was grim. 'We call it "the usual" because it's the one where all the accidents seem to happen on Sharp Edge.'

'Even to experienced climbers. And, as a recently diagnosed diabetic, he should know better than to take risks. I'll read him the riot act when I bring him round,' Mallory said. 'What about getting him to hospital afterwards?'

'The ambulance is going to meet us here. Should take him an hour to get to the hospital from here,' Rob said. 'Unless you think we need a helicopter?'

'Without seeing him, I can't tell. But it sounds like a straightforward hypoglycaemic coma, so we should be OK just with an ambulance. If I think otherwise when I see him, I'll radio you.'

Euan took her through the radio controls as Rob drove. The equipment was very similar to the sort Mallory had used before, so she quickly became familiar with it and could demonstrate it to Euan's satisfaction.

They were soon parked as near to the gully as they could get with the vehicle. Mallory strapped on the rescue harness, a triangle of material with straps which fastened through her legs and over her shoulders and clipped into a carabiner ring. Once they'd lowered her down to the ledge, it would be easy to transfer the harness to Ian and then the team at the top could haul him up, using a system of pulleys.

She put on a safety helmet, positioned her anchor carefully, clipped the self-braking belaying device—which would stop her falling too sharply—into place, made sure she had access to her medical equipment and radio, and then the team lowered her down to the ledge.

'Hi, I'm Mallory Ryman. You must be Martin,' she said to the grim-faced man on the ledge. 'And this is Ian, yes?'

Martin nodded. 'I should have kept a closer eye on him. I'm sorry, it's all my fault.'

Now wasn't the time to argue over blame. She had to bring Ian Cawsey round—and fast. Ian had already been out for a good twenty-five minutes. 'Did he hit his head or anything?'

Martin shook his head. 'He just said he felt dizzy. We were almost at the ledge, so I said we'd take a break. We made it here. Then he went all pale and sweaty and collapsed.'

'Thanks.' She used the radio to confirm the position to the team, then checked Ian's pulse. 'Fast.' She pricked his finger and did a quick blood sugar test. 'Way too low,' she said with a sigh. 'Martin, your friend's in a hypoglycaemic coma—that means there's not enough sugar in his blood. I can fix it, but I need to know if he had any seizures before he blacked out.'

Martin shook his head. 'No. He just felt dizzy.'

'Good. I'm going to give him some dextrose now. That should bring him round pretty quickly—five minutes, max.' She glanced at her watch and then located the vein on Ian's arm and injected the solution into it, following it up with a saline flush—the usual precaution to stop the dextrose leaking from the veins and causing irritation. And then she put him into the recovery position and crossed her fingers.

If this didn't work, she'd need to inject glucagon into a muscle to bring his blood sugar back up, and then dexamethasone to stop any potential swelling around the brain.

To her relief, before her five minutes were up, Ian opened his eyes. 'Wh—?' he began.

'Hello, Ian. Your blood sugar dropped too low,' Mallory said. 'You've been out of it for a while—scared your climbing partner, too.'

'I...'

'Here.' Mallory handed him a glucose drink. 'I'm going to tell the team you're conscious again—and then I think we need to have a word. Don't you?' She quickly confirmed to Rob that Ian had come round, they didn't need the helicopter and she'd be getting him ready for ascent in ten minutes. 'Now, Ian, you've been diagnosed fairly recently, so it's obviously type two or late onset diabetes—with type one, you'd have been diagnosed as a child and you'd be on insulin. A lot of people think that this means your diabetes is mild, but that's a myth—it can be just as dangerous as type one.'

'I'm sorry,' he muttered.

'Exercise is good for you—but if you have too much exercise, or you skip meals, or you don't eat enough carbohydrates, your blood sugar will drop rapidly and you'll go into a hypoglycaemic coma. Just as you did today,' she said. 'So you need to eat starchy foods, little and often, don't skip meals—particularly when you're climbing—and don't overdo things. Oh, and keep your glucose sweets in more than one place in case you lose some of them.'

Ian looked shamefaced. 'I'm sorry.'

'So you should be. Rob tells me you're an experienced climber. And it's lucky you weren't climbing on your own, or you wouldn't be here now. Do you know what happens if you go into a hypo and it's prolonged?'

'No.'

'Your brain tissues swell. Which means potential brain damage. Plus, if you're unconscious, there's the risk of choking. Not to mention falling and all the associated potential fractures—including breaking your neck. So you need to get to know your body's warning signs,' Mallory said. 'You might feel shaky or sweaty, your lips might tingle, your heart might pound and you might feel irritable or confused. If that happens, you need to have a sugary drink or some glucose tablets, and follow it up with a sandwich or something starchy like a cereal bar. It takes around fifteen minutes for the glucose or carbohydrate to affect your blood sugar levels, so just keep aware of how you're feeling. When you're climbing, you need increase your fluid intake and eat starchy food little and often.'

'So I don't have to stop climbing?'

'No. Just be sensible. The same if you have to drive long distances—stop and eat every two hours. And for heaven's sake don't climb on your own. If Martin hadn't been with you today, you could have been in real trouble. You might have fallen off the ledge and died.'

'I realise that now.'

'Good. I'm going to strap you into this harness, the lads are going to hoist you up and then it's off to hospital for you for a check-up.' She turned to Martin. 'Are you OK?'

'Relieved,' he admitted with a wry smile. 'I was panicking for a bit there.'

'Ian needs to be particularly careful now,' she said. 'If you're caught out overnight, and you don't have enough starchy food or glucose with you, this'll happen again.'

Martin nodded. 'I think we've both learned our lesson.'

'The hard way. Still, at least you're not going to forget it after this.' Mallory unclipped her safety harness, helped Ian into it, double-checked all the fastenings, then called Rob on the radio. 'Ready for you now,' she said.

*   *   *

This wasn't the same as the night Roly died, Will told himself. And Mallory had said she wasn't a risk-taker—unlike his twin. It was a straightforward enough rescue.

But…he couldn't help wondering if she was all right. He felt so *helpless*, stuck here. He couldn't even pace the room. It just wasn't the same with crutches. And drumming his fingers on the table didn't help either. Neither did listening to music. Or trying to catch up with professional journals. All he could think of was the second hand ticking slowly round the clock. Tick…tick…tick… So slowly, so the seconds seemed like hours.

Maybe he should have asked her to ring him. Let him know if she needed any medical back-up.

Maybe.

When the phone rang, he jumped with shock, then grabbed the cordless handset. 'Hello?' he barked into the receiver.

'Hi, Will. It's me,' Mallory said cheerily.

It was then he realised that he'd actually stopped breathing. Waiting for the news he didn't want to hear. The news that she'd been hurt, the same way Roly had been hurt.

'Just thought I'd let you know Ian's been taken off in the ambulance. The dextrose worked and he seems fine. I just want him checked over to be on the safe side. I read him the riot act—Martin Evans, too—and he's promised to be sensible in future.'

'Are you all right?' She sounded it, but he had to know.

'I'm fine. It's perfect weather for climbing.' Will could hear the smile in her voice. 'I don't know whether Ian was more embarrassed that he'd had to have the rescue team out, or angry with himself for missing out on the rest of his climb. But he's learned his lesson. Now, do you want me to pick up some wontons to go with our stir-fry?'

'You're really going to cook for me?'

'Don't think I'm going to make a habit of it. But, yeah, tonight. Let's celebrate one to us, nil to Sharp Edge. And I'm even going to let you have a glass of wine. So I'll see you in three-quarters of an hour. And I expect you to greet me with a smile, not a scowl. That's an order, not a request. *Ciao.*'

And she hung up.

Forty minutes later, she walked in. 'One bottle of chilled white wine,' she said, placing it in the fridge. 'Tiger prawns, ginger, lime and beansprouts. Noodles, wontons…' She looked at him. 'Actually, that was stupid of me. You're not going to manage noodles, are you?'

'I'm not a baby,' he said through gritted teeth.

'No, but you're wearing a cast.' She chuckled. 'I should have thought of that earlier. Damn. I don't do rice.'

'Takes too long, I suppose.'

'Yup. Anything over ten minutes is out. So, your choice. Cut-up noodles or no noodles?'

'I'm beginning to think I dislike you.'

'Could be worse. I could give you just one chopstick, see how you manage…'

Or she could feed them to him, bite by bite. Tempt him with every mouthful. He could almost imagine what it would be like, sitting with her in candlelight, feeding each other selected morsels before—

No. Absolutely not. Mallory was his locum, not his lover. He wasn't going to start thinking about her in that way. He lifted his chin. 'You're on an endorphin high.'

'Oh, yes,' she said with a grin. 'Endorphins. The body's natural opiates, released by exercise. And how!'

If she started nagging him now, he'd scream.

To his surprise, she didn't. She just smiled at him and said, 'Thanks.'

Will frowned. 'For what?'

'Ringing Rob Viner. Vouching for me.'

'Oh. That.'

'I'm not nagging you,' she began.

His jaw set. He knew that tone. 'You're a bad liar.'

'OK. So I *am* nagging you. You didn't tell me you used to assess applicants for the team. So what else did you do? Run first-aid training classes?'

'That's not relevant.'

'In other words, yes. And I bet that's all in the past, too.' She shook her head. 'Oh, Will, what do I have to do to make you see that life has to go on?'

'It's none of your business, Mallory.'

'Right. Then you're not going to be upset if I keep working with the team while I'm here, are you?'

He scowled at her. 'Stop nagging me, woman.'

'Then grow up and see sense.' She opened the bottle of wine, poured two glasses and handed him one. 'Now, before I start doing dinner—which is *not* cooking—we're going to have a toast. To Roly.'

She honestly expected him to toast his twin? After all he'd told her?

'To Roly,' she repeated, looking sternly at him.

'To Roly.' The words felt like splintered glass in his mouth.

'Now let him rest in peace. And stop torturing yourself.'

Before he could argue, she took a sip from her glass. 'Mmm. Gorgeous. I picked grapes on this estate in my gap year.'

He seized the change of subject gratefully. 'Before or after the sheep-shearing?'

'In between. How about you?'

He shook his head. 'I didn't bother with a gap year.'

'Shame. Mind you, when your cast's off and your leg's healed, you could try it then.'

'I'll pass. But tell me about it.'

'I went to Australia. Where I also learned about stir-fries.'

'Which isn't cooking,' he added.

Mallory laughed. 'You're learning!'

Not only was the stir-fry excellent, the company was good. Mallory made him laugh, entertained him with impersonations of the sheep-shearers she'd known and the temperamental chefs she'd washed up for—which was one of the reasons she hated washing up so much now—and taught him a lot he hadn't known about winemaking. Will couldn't remember the last time he'd enjoyed himself so much. Not even in Julie's company.

By the time they'd finished the wine and the tiny rice and seaweed crackers Mallory had bought as nibbles, both of them sprawled on the sofa with a soothing Bach cello concerto playing in the background, Will was tempted. More than tempted.

So he reached out and took her hand. Lifted it to his mouth. Kissed each fingertip in turn. And looked deep into her eyes.

Her pupils had expanded so much her eyes looked black. He didn't dare look any further down her body because he knew he'd see definite signs of arousal. And he also knew that she'd be able to see the same if she looked at him. Mallory Ryman turned him on more than any other woman he'd ever met, including Julie. She could drive him crazy with her nagging about the MR team, but...she drove him crazy in other ways, too. Much nicer ways.

He kissed her palm, then curled her fingers over the imprint of his kiss. 'What are we going to do about this thing between us, Mallory?'

She was silent for a long, long time. And then she made a face. 'Nothing. I don't do flings. And I'd bet serious money that you don't either.'

'No,' he admitted.

'Have you even been out with anyone, since it happened? On a proper date, I mean—not your meal out with Debbie.'

If she knew that hadn't been a real date, there was a good chance she'd guessed why, too. He rubbed the back of her hand with his thumb. 'No comment.'

'You mean just "no",' she said wryly.

'I haven't had time.'

'Because you've buried yourself in work.'

'I loved Julie,' he said quietly.

'Will, you have to let it go. You weren't the right one for her in the end. Maybe she wasn't the right one for you either.'

He was silent.

'I admit I'd like to go to bed with you, Will.' Her voice was husky. And way too sexy for his peace of mind. 'But I don't think it'd be good for either of us. I…I need to keep my work and my private life separate.'

There was something she wasn't telling him. His eyes narrowed. 'What are you really saying?'

'I'm saying it's a bad move. And I'm going to bed—upstairs, on my own—before we do something we both regret.' She leaned over and kissed him on the cheek. 'Goodnight, Will. And think about what I said. It's time to let the past go and move on.'

CHAPTER TEN

'I NEED your help, Dr Cooper,' Mallory announced a couple of days later.

'What's up? Paperwork?'

'No. Frank Wolsey. I went to see him today.'

'And he refused to talk to you?' Will guessed. 'I did warn you.'

'We have to do something, Will. Cathy Becker's under too much strain. Much more and she's in danger of having a nervous breakdown herself. And it'll be a vicious spiral. If she cracks, Frank'll feel guilty, it'll trigger another depressive episode for him, and then Cathy'll feel worse...' She shook her head with frustration. 'Somehow I've got to persuade her father to go to a day centre. Just a couple of times a week—that'll be enough to give Cathy and Mick a break. I tried phrasing it as a way of helping Cathy, but Frank wasn't having it.' She sighed. 'He's convinced himself it's the thin end of the wedge—if he agrees to go to day hospital, we'll have him in a home full time within a month.'

'It's a tough call.'

'He's stubborn, and pushing him's just going to make him even more determined to stay where he is.' Mallory crumbled a biscuit between her fingers. 'Maybe I should try it from the other way round. Supposing the day hospital needs his help, rather than him needing theirs?'

'So he thinks he's wanted and valued, rather than being shoved away in a corner?'

'Exactly. Low self-esteem's a problem with mental health—especially bipolar disease—and if we can do some-

117

thing about his self-esteem, he's more likely to take his medication properly instead of feeling that he doesn't deserve to have it.' She paused. 'And that's where I need your help. You know your patients better than I do. What kind of hobbies did he have? Or what did he do before he was retired?'

'He was a carpenter. Used to repair furniture in his spare time,' Will said.

'What if we got him to set up a woodwork class? That way he'd have to go to the hospital—and probably stay for lunch. And that might push him into realising that if other people enjoyed his classes, he might enjoy other people's classes.'

Will nodded. 'Good tactic, but you'd need to clear it with the day hospital first.'

She rolled her eyes. 'Which will take for ever. I know, I know, budgets and admin and the rest of it are important...but what about the patients? Don't their needs count any more?'

'I used to play squash with the day hospital's CEO,' Will said slowly.

Her face brightened. 'So you can use the old boy network to talk him round?'

He raised his eyebrows. 'I thought you'd disapprove of that sort of thing.'

'If it means my patients get what they need, I'll schmooze with the best of them,' Mallory said. 'I'd rather be climbing, but if slapping on a bit of make-up and wearing a short skirt and high heels will get my patients what they want, send me to the shoe shop right now!'

'There are two little reasons why I can't invite Paul to a game of squash,' he reminded her, nodding at his arm and leg.

'Then do lunch. Dinner. Whatever. I'll foot the bill. If he'll just agree to let us try...'

'It depends on a lot of other things. Insurance, for a start.'

Mallory groaned. 'I thought you were on my side?'

'I am. But we need to know the arguments against what we want, so we can come up with solutions before he can even raise the problems.'

Her eyes crinkled at the corner. 'You're a devious man, Will Cooper.'

'Get us some more coffee,' he said, 'and we'll brainstorm it. Though *you'll* have to do the writing.'

She chuckled. 'It's a deal. And if you pull this off, I'll keep you in chocolate biscuits for a year. That's a promise.'

A year. She was planning to stick around that long... Why did that make him feel as if the room was full of sunlight?

But the easiness between them didn't last for long. Will knew there was trouble brewing the minute Mallory walked through the door. Her face was set, her generous mouth was compressed into a thin line and she banged her doctor's bag down on the table.

'What's happened?' he asked.

She gave a derisive laugh. 'I don't know how you have the hide to ask that one, Will Cooper. You know damn well what's happened.'

Er—no. He didn't. He frowned. 'You've lost me there, Mallory.'

'Don't act dumb with me! If you don't trust me as a doctor, fine—but I'd prefer you to say it to my face than go sneaking round behind my back, checking up on me.'

His frown deepened. 'I haven't been checking up on you.'

'No? Then perhaps you can explain why Greg Foulger rang the surgery to ask for antibiotics for eczema. Saying it was on your advice. I'd already prescribed a moderately potent steroid cream to clear it up.'

'Greg didn't say he'd been to see you.'

'So you *did* ring him.'

'No. He rang me.'

Mallory folded her arms. 'Why?'

'Because he's had it before. You know yourself that discoid eczema is recurrent.'

She did—it was also known as nummular eczema, where itchy, symmetrical coin-shaped lesions appeared on the limbs. The patient tended to be male, either middle-aged or elderly. There was no known cause and it usually cleared up spontaneously in two weeks.

'You probably told him all about it,' he continued, 'but I assumed he was ringing me simply because he'd had it before so he knew what it was. He wanted to know if he could use the same cream rather than have to pay for another prescription. He's on a tight budget and he's not entitled to free prescriptions,' Will said. 'And you also know that secondary infection's quite common, particularly in a recurring episode.'

'Hence the need for antibiotics. I did tell him to come back if he hadn't noticed any improvement in a couple of days or if any of the discs became inflamed.' Mallory bit her lip. 'So the patients don't trust me either.'

'No, it's just that he's getting on a bit so he's set in his ways, he's used to me and he just rang me for advice. If he'd told me he'd already seen you, I would have told him to go back to see you.'

'He's not the only one who rang you either, is he?' She listed four other patients she knew had asked his advice. After seeing her.

'Mallory, nobody's checking up on you. I trust you completely. But this is a community. I can't stop patients ringing me, can I?'

'You haven't exactly put them off, though, have you?'

He flushed. 'OK. Guilty as charged. Yes, I've talked to

any patient who called here, given them an impromptu consultation instead of telling them to ring the surgery.'

'Why?'

'Because,' he said, 'I'm *bored*. I'm sick of being stuck in here, not able to do my job.' Because his job was who he was. He was Dr Will Cooper, Darrowthwaite's senior GP. Without that…

She rolled her eyes. 'Will, you were hit by a car. Fractures take time to heal. You *know* that. You said yourself that you can't write out prescriptions or drive out to a house call. You can't examine a patient one-handed and you certainly mustn't put any weight on that leg yet.'

'I know all that. But I'm still bored.'

'And you need to rest while your bones heal. I can't wave a magic wand and make them knit together overnight. What do you expect me to do about it?'

Now, that was a leading question. And he could think of several ways Mallory could take his mind off his boredom. Starting with a kiss…

No. He really had to stop his mind thinking along those lines. 'I'm sorry,' he muttered.

'Hey.' She switched the kettle on. 'Me, too. I shouldn't have leapt to conclusions.'

'Understandable. And you're right. I should rest.'

'And it's driving you mad.' She sat down next to him. 'You want to be out there, helping patients. Because your work isn't just a job to you, is it? It's who you are. Dr Will Cooper.'

'I didn't realise it showed so much.'

'It does, to me,' she said softly. 'Well, maybe we can do something about that. There are some circumstances where you don't need to update records and you don't need to fill out prescriptions.' She gave him a thoughtful look. 'You have two baby clinics a week, right?'

'Yes.'

'At Charles's practice we used to have a rota for the baby clinics—one of us would give the mums a quick ten-minute talk on that week's topic, something like teething or weaning or sleep problems, and then we'd be there for another twenty minutes or so to help the health visitor answer any of the worries that new mums have but think they're too trivial to take to the surgery.'

'Preventative medicine. So if I help with the queries now, it'll stop the little worries turning into real medical problems a couple of months down the line.'

'Exactly.' She smiled. 'You can do the whole thing sitting down, the health visitor will take care of weight and length measurements, and you don't need to write anything down, so your leg and arm can still get some rest.'

'The next baby clinic's tomorrow. I'd better ring the health visitor now, then.'

She passed him the cordless phone. 'If you ring now, you'll probably get her before she goes out on home visits.'

'You're right. Thanks.' Yet again she'd proved what a good doctor she was—spotting the problem and coming up with a solution that worked. Because she'd clearly realised if his frustration or boredom grew any more, he'd be tempted to try his leg and arm before they were ready, damaging them further and causing himself an even longer wait until he was fit.

Mallory was a real asset to the practice. And if she only wanted to work part time and spend the rest of her time climbing, he could definitely make a place for her at the surgery. He ignored the little voice that added, *And in your life.*

In the early hours of the morning the phone shrilled. Mallory groaned, rolled over and grabbed the receiver. 'Dr Ryman.'

'Doctor, I'm so sorry to wake you—but it's my little

Maisie. She's got a really high temperature and I just can't get it down.'

Mallory sat up, struggling to clear her head. 'Maisie.'

'Maisie Foster. I'm Gillian, her mother.'

'Sorry.' Mallory squinted at the clock. It was nearly half past two. 'OK. How old is she?'

'Two.'

'And how long's she had the temperature?'

'Just tonight. She's had that bug that's going round nursery.'

There were a couple of bugs circulating the town—a lingering cough, sickness and diarrhoea, and a virus that caused a very high temperature. It sounded as if Maisie had been unlucky enough to get one on top of the other. 'Have you given her any infant paracetamol?'

'I tried, but she threw it back up. Oh, my God! No!'

'What's happening?'

'She's— I think she's having a fit.' Gillian's voice was shaky. 'She just went rigid and now her eyes have rolled back and her legs and arms are twitching.'

'That's her body's reaction to a very high temperature— it's called a febrile convulsion. I know it looks scary, but most of the time they're really not serious. Try not to worry—I'll be with you very shortly. Do you know what the recovery position is?'

'Yes.'

'Good. Put Maisie in the recovery position. When she's conscious again—that's likely to be some time in the next five minutes—she'll probably go straight into a deep sleep. I want you to take her sheets and blankets off, strip her down to her vest and nappy and sponge her with lukewarm water. Let the water dry on her skin and that will help to bring her temperature down. And it has to be *lukewarm* water, Gillian,' she emphasised. 'Cold water'll make things worse. Try to stay calm—I'm on my way out to you.' She took Gillian's address and directions to the house, hung up and dragged herself into her clothes. Then she tiptoed down the stairs, not wanting to wake Will. Hopefully he hadn't heard the phone ring as she'd taken the cordless receiver upstairs with her and the base unit didn't make a sound.

Just as she was about to leave the house, the living-room door opened. Will stood there, leaning on his crutches, his hair dishevelled.

He was wearing just an old T-shirt and a pair of shorts. 'Sexily rumpled' didn't even begin to describe him. Mallory had to drag her eyes away from his legs. She definitely needed the draught of cold air by the front door to keep her libido in check.

'What's up?' he asked.

'Maisie Foster. Febrile convulsions. I'll try not to wake you when I get back,' she said.

'Do you want me to come with you?'

'No, it's OK. Gillian gave me directions. Besides, you need to rest.' Plus they both knew that it would take a while for Will to get dressed—and Maisie's mother needed a doctor's support and reassurance as soon as possible.

Though when Mallory did get back, an hour later, Will's light was on.

'You should be resting,' she said.

'Yeah, yeah. You've done that lecture already. Several times.'

'And you clearly don't listen,' she retorted.

'I've been resting all day. Anyway, I couldn't sleep. How's Maisie?'

'Holding her own. I gave her an infant paracetamol suppository to bring her temperature down and some diazepam to stop the fitting,' Mallory said. 'I'm fairly sure it's just this virus doing the rounds—Gillian knew of a couple of other children at nursery who'd had exactly the same thing.

But because it's Maisie's first ever febrile convulsion I've told Gillian to take her to hospital first thing in the morning so they can check her out. I've given her a letter and I'll ring the paediatric assessment unit to let them know she's coming.'

'Spot on,' Will told her.

'Want a hot drink?'

'Cooking for me again?' he teased.

'Warming milk in the microwave doesn't count as cooking. Have you got any cinnamon?'

'Nope.'

'Cocoa?' she tried.

'Nope.'

'Then I guess it's plain hot milk or plain hot milk.'

Will followed her into the kitchen, manoeuvred himself into a chair and rested his crutches against the table. 'Sorry you got called out. Maybe I should have switched everything through to a night service.'

'I'm your locum,' she reminded him. 'I knew that night call-outs were a possibility before I agreed to stay on. They don't happen that often.'

'No.' Will accepted the hot milk gratefully. 'Thanks.'

'So why can't you sleep? Leg hurting? Arm?'

'No. I'm just awake.' He wasn't going to tell her the truth. That he was awake because he'd been thinking about her. Thinking about how life had settled into a regular pattern, with Mallory working at the surgery in the morning, doing house calls two afternoons a week and climbing on the other afternoons. He'd taken up her suggestion of working at the baby clinics, which was just enough to stop him getting bored and take him to his limits of tiredness. She did mountain rescue training twice a week, and he'd timed the Indian take-away order for fifteen minutes after she came home, enough time for her to shower before their meal.

They'd quietly slipped into a routine—and Will liked it. Correction. He liked having Mallory around. Though if he had any sense, he'd stop this right now before he got in too deep. Because they didn't have a future. She wasn't the domestic goddess he needed, and he wasn't going to join her back in the mountains.

'Penny for them?'

Their gazes met. Will couldn't help looking at her mouth. Her warm, beautifully shaped mouth. And remembering what it was like to taste it. Properly.

'You'd better get some sleep. You've got surgery in the morning,' he said. Though he wished he hadn't said it. Mallory and bed in the same thought was dangerous. Way too dangerous. 'I'll see you in the morning,' he said gruffly, leaving his half-drunk hot milk and limping out of the room on his crutches before he did something unforgivable.

Like asking her to go to bed with him.

CHAPTER ELEVEN

THE following week, Mallory was studying a journal and making notes. Will was watching her surreptitiously from behind his own journal. She'd ruffled her auburn hair so it stuck up even more and her tongue was just protruding from between her lips as she concentrated on her reading. She looked just like a mischievous elf.

Not to mention incredibly sexy. It was just as well he couldn't put any weight on his leg or he'd have been over there next to her in a nanosecond.

And then the light flickered and died.

Mallory put her notepad inside the journal to mark her page and stood up. 'Where's your fuse box?'

'I don't think it's the fuses. It's probably a power cut,' Will said. 'We tend to get them when it's windy. And the forecast was for strong winds this afternoon.'

She frowned. 'Oh, great. Just when I wanted to catch up on my reading. How long do they usually last?'

He shrugged. 'Anything from a few minutes to a couple of hours.'

She walked over to the window and peered out. 'I hadn't realised how strong the wind had got. And the lights are off all down the street so it's not just a pocket—looks as if we might be having sandwiches instead of pizza for dinner tonight.' She sighed. 'Oh, well. Better get prepared in case I'm called out. I've got a torch in my car. Have you got one indoors?'

'Yep. And there should be some candles in the kitchen, in the middle drawer under the draining board.'

'Matches?'

'But no camping stove. I gave all my equipment to charity. And Roly's.'

She nodded, as if understanding why he'd done it, though the look on her face told him she didn't approve. 'I'll grub out the candles,' she said.

She returned, two minutes later, holding two half-used candles. 'For someone who has a lot of power cuts, you're not exactly well prepared, are you? I'd better go and buy some.'

Will turned from the window. 'It's blowing a gale out there, Mallory. It's stupid to take risks, going out when you don't really have to. It's not that dark yet. We'll manage.'

But they had no idea how long the power was going to be out. The candles weren't going to last for long.

'I'll ring the power company,' Mallory suggested. Except the line was busy. Every time she pressed the redial button she looked more annoyed, banged the phone down and said it was engaged again.

'It's probably affected the whole of Darrowthwaite,' Will said. 'There might be news on the radio.'

'Except we need electricity for the radio to work,' Mallory pointed out.

'The one in the kitchen runs on batteries.'

'I hope your stock of batteries is better than your stock of candles,' Mallory said, and went into the kitchen to check.

It wasn't. But at least the radio worked. For now.

'How old are the batteries in this?' Mallory asked.

Will shrugged. 'No idea.'

'So they could go at any time, too.' She frowned. 'The radio station'll probably give us an update on the hour as part of the local news so we'd better conserve the batteries for the news reports.'

'Sorry,' Will said.

'I can't believe you're this disorganised. You're a GP,

for goodness' sake! And you used to be part of the MR team. How can you be like this now?'

He scowled. 'It'll be over in a few minutes. Don't make such a fuss.'

Except he was wrong. Four hours later, they still had no power. Mallory made them both a sandwich, supplementing it with fruit, a carton of orange juice and a large packet of chocolate biscuits in lieu of a pot of coffee.

The news broadcast at nine o'clock hinted that power might not be restored until the following morning.

Mallory shivered. 'Oh, wonderful. So we just sit here and freeze.' When Will chuckled, she glared at him. 'What's so funny?'

'This is the woman who wants to climb Everest. And you're whinging about the cold.'

'That's different. In the Himalayas I'd be prepared for the cold and the altitude. This is Cumbria. The UK. It's not *meant* to be this cold.'

'Mallory, it's not that bad.'

'Yes, it is. I'm *freezing*! And because your gas central heating needs electricity for the system's clock to work, we've got no heating as well as no light. We can't make a hot drink, we're down to our last candle *and* there's no guarantee the power will be back on in the morning.'

'Someone's having caffeine withdrawal symptoms,' he teased.

'Too right. But the whole town's out so I can't even go out and get some coffee.'

'And it's too dangerous to be out in this anyway.' Will's good humour faded. 'I hope no one's stupid enough to go climbing in this.'

'I'm *sure* no one's that stupid,' Mallory said, 'because that wouldn't be a challenge. It'd be reckless.'

'Fancy another game of Scrabble by candlelight?'

'No. And I'm not playing snap with you either. You

cheat.' She scowled. 'I can't even have a hot-water bottle because we can't boil water. Why couldn't you have had a gas cooker or an Aga?'

'Asks the woman who doesn't do cooking.' Will paused. There were spare blankets in the airing cupboard. All he had to do was tell her to take the torch, go upstairs and get what she needed to keep her warm. Except his mouth wasn't working in synch with his common sense, because what came out was, 'You know how you'd keep warm up a mountain.'

She nodded. 'In a tent. In a heavy duty sleeping bag.'

Will's mouth was really running away with him. 'How about in a sofa bed under two duvets? Being the next best thing to a tent and sleeping bag?'

Her jaw dropped. 'You're asking me to sleep with you?'

Oh, yes. But not quite in the way he really wanted. 'Mallory, I have one arm in plaster and a pinned leg. I'm hardly in a position to ruin your honour, if that's what you're worrying about. All I'm suggesting is an early night—to save candle power—and sharing a little body heat to keep warm. It's the sensible thing.'

Mallory wasn't quite so sure. Incapacitated or not, Will Cooper was still one hell of an attractive man. She already knew how he kissed, and the memory alone was enough to make her pulse race. Sharing a bed with him was going to be dangerous. More than dangerous.

On the other hand, she was freezing. The cold would be enough to keep her common sense in place.

'OK.' She pulled the sofa bed out and made it up. 'I'll, er, get my duvet while you, um, change,' she said.

Hopefully the light from the candle was too dim for him to see her blushing. Really! This was ridiculous. She wasn't that far off thirty, she wasn't a virgin, and in her job she was used to seeing the male form in various stages of undress and it didn't faze her in the slightest. So how come she was feeling all awkward and shy now? Why was she reacting like this to the idea of sleeping next to Will, who'd be clothed anyway—albeit in a T-shirt and loose shorts?

She didn't want to know the answer to that one. She simply fled upstairs, changed into her pyjamas and grabbed the duvet.

The teddy bears on her pyjamas were obvious, even in the candlelight. But Will didn't laugh. Well, not out loud. Mallory was convinced that, if she dared to look him in the eye, she'd see a twinkle there.

But her mouth dried as she saw Will lying under the duvet, on the left-hand side of the sofa bed.

Because this wasn't a situation she could deal with.

Will was waiting for her to get into bed with him.

She shivered, and Will clearly assumed it was because she was cold because he patted the space next to him. 'Chuck the other duvet on top and cuddle into me,' he said. 'You'll soon get warm again.' When she hesitated, he added, 'Just think of it as an MR exercise.'

Now, that she couldn't do. She was much too aware of him as a man.

'I'm cold as well,' he said softly. 'And that's not good for my leg.'

'Of all the excuses!' she spluttered.

But he'd lightened the mood, and she climbed into bed beside him. The extra duvet didn't seem to make much difference so she gave in and cuddled into him, grateful for his bodily warmth.

'Sweet dreams,' Will said.

'Yeah.'

Mallory was sure she was never going to fall asleep. She was too keyed up, thrown off balance by Will's nearness. And yet it was in the small hours of the morning when she woke. She was still curled into Will—but his T-shirt had ridden up during the night and now her left cheek was resting directly against his chest, with the light sprinkling of hairs tickling her skin.

His top wasn't the only one that had ridden up. So had her pyjama jacket. And Will's hand was flat against her back, holding her close.

Holding her like a lover.

She could hardly breathe. And then she felt his fingers move against her back. Very slightly. Hardly perceptible. But she knew that he, too, was awake.

The tension in his body matched hers. Both of them were lying still, almost as if afraid to make the first move. Afraid that the other would make the first move.

Stop now, she told herself. Pretend you're asleep. Don't respond.

Her fingertips weren't listening. They were moving in tiny, tiny circles at the edge of his waist. Reflecting the circles his fingertips were making against her own skin.

And then she felt Will's lips against her hair. Gentle. Questioning, not demanding. She could stop this any time she chose.

She ought to stop it right now. She knew that. But she couldn't help herself. She shifted slightly and tipped her face up towards his.

And then Will kissed her. What started out as sweet and gentle suddenly turned explosive, demanding, and she kissed him back.

That was when the trouble really started. Because kissing wasn't enough. She found herself peeling off his T-shirt— and helping him remove her pyjamas, too, because he was hampered by his cast.

'Ah, Mallory, I need to touch you,' he whispered, his voice hoarse and cracked with wanting.

'Your leg…' she remembered belatedly.

'Please.'

He'd asked nicely. How could she refuse?

Who was she trying to kid? She wasn't doing him any favours. She wanted this every bit as much as he did. Had wanted it from the moment she'd first seen him, a second before she'd switched into doctor mode and started tending his wounds. And that was half the reason why she spent as much of her free time as possible climbing. So she didn't give into temptation.

Though that was exactly what she was doing now. And she couldn't stop herself.

She shifted so that she was straddling him. 'I'm not hurting you?'

'Only in the nicest possible way.' There was amusement in his voice, as well as sheer lust. And then he gasped as she moved against him. 'Mallory…I want to make love with you.'

Well, she already knew that. The evidence was very, very noticeable from where she was sitting.

His thumbs brushed the hard peaks of her nipples, and she gave an 'Mmm' of pleasure.

'You can say no if you want to.' Passion slurred his words.

'Yes.'

He stopped touching her immediately. 'I'm sorry. I'll respect your wishes.'

'No, I mean *yes*, yes,' she said.

'Ah. *Yes,* yes.' He slid his uninjured hand round the back of her neck. 'Tell me,' he invited.

'I want you, too,' she said huskily. And reached down to kiss him.

When she broke the kiss he murmured in protest and reached up to kiss her again. And again.

The next thing she knew, they were both naked. She had no idea when they'd finished removing their clothes, who had done it or even *how* they'd done it, given the cast on his left arm and his pinned right leg. Mallory couldn't think straight. Will's clean male scent made her dizzy and the way he was touching her made her want more and more. The ultimate closeness.

'Now,' she said.

Will sighed in pleasure as she moved over him. 'Oh, yes. You don't know how much I've wanted this.'

Yes, she did. Because she'd felt exactly the same.

And then she stopped thinking as he drove her higher and higher towards the peak. She heard him cry out her name, heard her own answering cry, and then both his arms were round her, holding her close. Cradling her tenderly.

Neither of them said a word. But her head was buried in his shoulder and his lips were against the exposed curve of her neck. When she finally moved and settled down by his side, he was still holding her tightly, and her arms were just as tight around him. And as she drifted to sleep, Mallory had the strangest feeling that at last she'd come home.

CHAPTER TWELVE

MALLORY was having the most amazing dream. She was warm and secure, lying in the arms of the man she loved.

Loved?

She blinked. And that was when she realised that she wasn't dreaming. She was awake. Her head was still pillowed on Will's chest, his arm was firmly wrapped round her and his hand settled on the curve of her hip.

The man she loved.

No. No, no, and treble no. Of *course* she wasn't in love with Will Cooper. She couldn't be. It was impossible.

But…she was in bed with him. You couldn't have got so much as a blade of grass between their naked bodies right now. And last night, they'd made love.

How could she have been so stupid? She'd known Will was off limits…and still she'd made love with him. She almost groaned aloud. How on earth was she going to get out of this mess without hurting Will?

Mallory's eyes were tightly shut but Will knew she was awake. He'd felt her body stiffen against his just for a moment.

He'd just done the most stupid thing in his life.

Hadn't he promised himself he'd keep his distance? But no. She'd curled up against him last night, purely for the sake of warmth…and he hadn't been able to stop himself. He'd woken with her in his arms and he'd wanted her.

OK, she'd been there with him all the way. She'd said yes. She'd been just as carried away as he'd been. But this morning was a whole new ball game. He didn't have a clue what the rules were or how to play.

Then there was a loud 'click', music filled the room and the lights came on.

'Houston, we have power,' Mallory murmured.

'Yup.'

There was a long, excruciating pause.

He'd been the one to start it. He'd been the one to suggest sharing a bed, purely for warmth's sake. So he was the one who had to break the ice now. 'Good morning,' Will said softly.

'Good morning.'

He could hear the wariness in her voice, though he didn't dare shift so he could see her face. Not yet. Because he didn't want to see rejection or pity in her eyes. He sighed. 'We're going to have to face it, you know. Last night happened.'

'Power cut. Cold. Propinquity,' Mallory said.

So it hadn't meant anything to her? OK. He could cope with that. Even though it hurt more than his leg and his arm and his head had all rolled into one. If that was the way she wanted it, he'd make it easy for her. Pretend it hadn't meant anything to him either. 'I'm glad you think so, too. I'd hate…what happened to change things between us.'

'We're still colleagues. Housemates,' Mallory agreed.

He wasn't sure if that was good or bad right now. And then it hit him. 'Um, last night… Sorry to harp on about this, but…we didn't take any precautions.'

'No.'

They'd both been too carried away. Too needy. Too urgent.

'I'm sorry. Um, what I'm trying to say is…' Oh, hell. Where was his eloquence when he needed it? Deserted him at the same time as his common sense, it seemed. 'Look, if there are, um, any consequences…I'll do the right thing by you.'

Was that a shudder of horror or a hastily suppressed giggle he'd felt running through her? His eyes narrowed. 'Mallory?'

'Uh-huh.' Her voice wasn't quite normal but he had no way of knowing what she was feeling. Unless he looked at her. Which he really, really didn't want to do.

'I'm fairly sure it's a safe time,' she said. 'And, um, despite last night, I don't think either of us sleeps around.'

'No.' She hadn't dated anyone else since she'd been here, had she? And then he had a really nasty thought. He hadn't heard her call anyone and she hadn't had any post since she'd been staying with him, but that didn't mean a thing. Maybe she'd had her post delivered to the surgery. And she had a mobile phone—there was always texting. Or email. More than one way to stay in touch with someone special… 'I hope this doesn't cause any trouble between you and your—' his voice cracked '—man.'

She went rigid then, and he felt something shatter inside. Hope. So she *did* have someone waiting for her down in the New Forest. She wasn't the free spirit he'd thought she was—*hoped* she was.

'There's no one to cause trouble with.'

It took a few moments to sink in, and if he hadn't been lying flat on his back he'd have fallen over. There wasn't anyone else? Well, *duh,* he told himself. Of course there wasn't. She wouldn't have made love with him last night if she was involved with someone else. Mallory Ryman had integrity in spades. And he'd just insulted her by suggesting otherwise.

'I'm supposed to be in surgery in half an hour,' Mallory said.

Will glanced at the clock on the mantelpiece. She was

right. What would a friend and colleague and housemate do now?

What he *really* wanted to do was bend his head and kiss her. Make love with her again. But this time he knew she'd push him away. So he had to take the sensible option and pretend none of this had ever happened. 'Want me to make coffee while you have a shower?'

'Thanks, but you can't fill the kettle one-handed. Not safely anyway. I'll sort it.' She sat up, and Will couldn't help glancing at her. Lord, her back was beautiful. Creamy skin, the perfect shape. If she let her hair grow, it would stream down her back in the perfect contrast. And then he'd play with the ends of her beautiful, silky hair and stroke her back and…

As if she sensed his gaze and the way his thoughts were heading—and she'd already wrapped the top duvet around her front, he noticed—she pulled the duvet round her fully, sarong-style, and wriggled out of the sofa bed. 'I'll, um, let you get dressed in peace.'

Meaning, get some clothes on so I don't have to face what we did, Will interpreted. 'OK.'

By the time Mallory came into the kitchen fifteen minutes later, Will was fully dressed and composed. 'I've put some toast on. Though you'll have to butter it yourself.'

'Thanks.' She coughed. 'I don't have time for coffee, but I'll make you one.' She switched the kettle on, then headed for the door again. 'I'll just turn your bed back into the sofa before I go.'

'Cheers.'

This was terrible. Last night… Oh, how could she have been so stupid? Mallory berated herself as she sorted out the living room. The sheets on the sofa bed were crumpled. Extremely crumpled. And she flushed as she remembered how they'd got that way.

Hell. There was only one way out of this. She had to explain to Will about Geoff. Find him a new locum. And leave, before she really hurt him.

She put the bedding in the washing machine, made him a coffee, then nerved herself to face him.

'Will…I think we need to talk.'

'Nothing to talk about. Last night was just…one of those things.'

One of those things, one of those flings. But they'd already discussed that. And they'd agreed—no fling.

'Thank you,' she said softly. She buttered her toast, then started crumbling it onto her plate. 'Will, I haven't been entirely honest with you.'

That got his attention. One very blue stare met hers. 'How do you mean?'

'About there not being anyone else.' She paused. 'There was.'

'Was,' he repeated, his face unreadable.

He wasn't going to make this easy for her. Not that she deserved it. She sighed. 'I was…involved with another of the doctors at my practice. It was one of those things—you start out as friends, go out together as friends and then something changes.'

'I see.'

Mixing work and relationships. And she'd just made the same mistake all over again. She forced herself to continue. 'Geoff's a great doctor, he's kind and funny and sweet and a great catch. Good-looking—the sort of man any woman would dream about.' Any woman with half a brain. And right now Mallory was convinced she didn't even have a quarter of a brain working. 'But he doesn't do mountains. And…he asked me to marry him.'

Will said nothing. Absolutely nothing.

Well, what was he supposed to say? Give her a hug and say, 'Never mind, it doesn't matter?' Hardly.

'I had no idea. Well, I did. I knew his feelings were stronger than mine. I just…' This was getting worse and worse and worse. 'I liked him very much. Loved him even—but only as a friend. I was trying to cool things down between us, and then…' She sighed. 'I really wasn't expecting him to propose. Marrying Geoff would have been a disaster for both of us. I couldn't be the safe, domesticated woman he wanted me to be. Saying no hurt him terribly, and I felt bad about it because I cared about him— but saying yes would have hurt him more in the long run.' She swallowed. 'I made a huge mess of things, Will. And because I didn't have my mind properly on the job—because I was upset about hurting Geoff—I nearly killed one of my patients.'

'Lindy.'

'Yes.' She steeled herself. 'Something else you should know. Geoff is Charles's son.'

She could hear the kitchen clock ticking. Very, very slowly. And very, very loudly—almost as loud as the blood pounding in her ears.

'Your father's best friend.'

'So I didn't just hurt Geoff. I hurt Charles, too. And my father. He'd been planning…I dunno, almost a dynasty, a merger between our families. Geoff's a bit of a traditionalist—before he proposed, he actually asked my father's permission. Dad was delighted. I think he started planning his father-of-the-bride speech right then and there. Except I ruined it all by saying no.'

'I see.' Cool and calm. And Will's face was absolutely unreadable.

'I asked Geoff to go climbing with me so he could understand why I do it. But he didn't enjoy it. He couldn't see what all the fuss was about. When I told him I wanted to climb Everest one day, he thought I was joking.' She bit her lip. 'I suppose the real problem was that I didn't love him. Not in the right way.' She took a deep breath. 'I'm sorry. I've let you down, too. I'll—I'll stay on until you find another locum, then leave.'

'No need.' He shrugged. 'Last night…was a mistake. But we needn't let it get in the way of business.'

A cold, hard knot formed in Mallory's throat. Business. That wasn't quite…

Yes, it was. It was *exactly* how she should see things between herself and Will. Business, with possible friendship only as a secondary consideration.

'We've got on fine as colleagues, as housemates. Why change things now?'

'You're absolutely right.' She glanced at the clock. 'I'd better be off, or Marion'll put me in detention for being late. Anything you want me to bring back at lunchtime?'

He shook his head. 'No, I'm fine, thanks.'

She gave him a quick smile. 'See you later, then.'

'*Ciao.*'

At the surgery, she feigned a brightness she didn't feel when she saw her first patient. 'Good morning, Mrs Montgomery. What can I do for you?'

'It's…' Roisin Montgomery sighed. 'I'm probably being silly. But I'm convincing myself that I'm going through the menopause—and I'm only thirty-five!'

'You're probably a bit on the young side,' Mallory said. 'I'd give you another ten years, yet. What kind of symptoms have you been having?'

Roisin shook her head. 'Nothing I can really pin down. I've been feeling a bit hot—I wondered if it was hot flushes. I haven't got much energy and I just feel a bit off colour—a bit sick and I ache all over. Plus, I've been getting a lot of headaches lately, though Phillip says it's because I'm putting in too many hours at work.' She shrugged. 'I've always suffered from headaches anyway.'

Mallory looked at her patient. Roisin was wearing full make-up so Mallory couldn't check out her suspicions about a skin rash but, given the other symptoms that Roisin had described, there was a possibility... 'Roisin, have you lost weight recently? Gone off your food at all?'

'Well—yes, I have. But I could do with losing a few pounds anyway.'

'What about your skin? Anything different there?'

'I've had to change my make-up. A few months ago my face really reacted—I came out in huge red blotches. Then it went away again.'

Mallory nodded. It was beginning to sound like systemic lupus erythematosus or SLE—the symptoms tended to die down and flare up again periodically. 'They wouldn't have been on your cheeks and across the bridge of your nose, by any chance?'

'Yes.' Roisin rolled her eyes. 'Phillip—my partner—said it looked a bit like a butterfly. But he's an artist—trust him to make it into a pattern!'

'What about your hair—anything different there?'

'There's been a bit more than usual on my hairbrush, but that's probably stress. Work's been a bit mad lately.'

'How about your eyes?'

'I had to give up wearing contact lenses—they made my eyes feel scratchy. But again it could be just because I'm spending too much time on the computer at work.'

Stress and overwork were possible explanations for Roisin's symptoms—but the rash made Mallory think otherwise. 'I'm pretty sure you're not going through the menopause,' Mallory said. 'I need to do some blood tests to check, but from what you've just told me I think you might have a disease called SLE, or lupus.'

'Lupus? But that's fatal, isn't it?'

'No—not nowadays. Most patients have a completely normal life expectancy and we can keep the disease under control, though there's no cure,' Mallory said. 'All it means is that your body's immune system is overactive and produces too many antibodies, which attack the tissues around your joints and affect your blood—and that in turn affects the rest of your body. It's actually pretty common—probably around one in a thousand women get it. You'll find that sometimes it flares up and other times you'll be in remission and feel a lot better.'

'What causes it?'

'We don't know,' Mallory said. 'There's no evidence of a virus or infectious cause, though you might find you feel worse just before your period so there may be a hormonal link. The good news is, if it is what I think, we can keep your symptoms under control—I can give you some drugs to calm your immune system down and stop the inflammation. Depending on what the tests show me, I might prescribe steroids to calm your system down, or I might just give you some aspirin.'

'Aspirin?'

'Unless you're sensitive to it?'

Roisin shook her head. 'Not that I know of.'

'Good. You'll need to use sunscreen and sunblock to stop the rash coming back, because it tends to be made worse by sunlight. And you might be a bit anaemic at the moment—that'd explain the tiredness. If the blood tests show your red blood cell count's a bit low, I can give you iron tablets.'

'Is it catching?'

'No.' Mallory smiled. 'There's no worry that you'll pass it to your partner or any of your colleagues.'

'But—why me?'

'Sorry, I don't have an answer to that,' Mallory said. 'There might be a genetic element to it, but we just don't know enough about the disease right now. As well as the blood test, I want to check your blood pressure and I'd like you to give me a urine sample—SLE can cause kidney problems, but if we pick it up early we can treat it more effectively. The same goes for lung problems.'

'What about having children? I mean, Phillip and I waited until my career was more off the ground. Have we left it too late?'

'No, not at all. Years ago, patients with lupus were advised not to have babies, but we know more about the disease now. You can still try for a baby if you want to,' Mallory said. 'Though obviously we'll need to keep a much closer eye on you than on the average mum, and we can't use certain drugs because they can affect the baby. There's a small chance you'll have a flare-up after you've had the baby.' There was also a greater risk of prematurity and of the mother suffering from pre-eclampsia. 'There's also a possibility that you have antiphospholipid syndrome—or Hughes' syndrome—that's when your blood's "sticky". We can do a blood test to check, and if that's the case we'll need to give you low-dose aspirin to make sure you don't have a miscarriage.'

'Will the baby get it?'

'Probably not. The baby might get a skin rash from the antibodies in your blood, though that will clear up after the birth.'

Roisin shook her head, as if clearing it. 'So what happens now?'

'I'd like to take a blood sample and send it for what's called an ANA or anti-nuclear antibody test—around 90 to 95 per cent of patients with lupus have a positive test. If that's positive, I'll ask for a DNA antibody test, which will tell me whether it definitely is lupus and how active the disease is.'

Roisin bit her lip. 'It's a lot to take in.'

'I know. And if you want to talk to me at any time about

it or bring your partner to see me, that's fine,' Mallory said. 'It might not be that.'

'But you think it probably is.'

'From the rash you described, yes.'

'Will I have to go to hospital?'

'If it is lupus, I'd like you to go to a regular clinic,' Mallory said. 'And there are some support groups that can help put you in touch with others who have lupus and can tell you more about their experiences.' She flicked through a book and wrote down a couple of names and phone numbers. 'These are the helpline numbers, or you can check out their web sites.'

'Thanks.'

'One thing I would say—check with us before you use any complementary medicine, especially if you're thinking about dietary supplements or herbal remedies, because there's a possibility they might react with the drugs we prescribe for you. You might find aromatherapy helps but don't massage any inflamed or swollen areas, and you need to be careful about which oils you use—the citrus oils, particularly bergamot, are photosensitising, and might react badly with your skin.'

Mallory took a blood sample. 'I'll have the results back in a few days. I'll ask Mrs Prentiss to give you a ring when they're back, and then you can come and have another chat with me. Bring Phillip with you, if you like.'

'I'll do that,' Roisin said. 'Thanks, Dr Ryman.'

The rest of Mallory's surgery that morning was more routine. And then it was time to go back and face Will. Climbing wasn't an option today—he'd know that she was just being a coward and avoiding him. Besides, it was damp and cloudy, not her favourite conditions for climbing. Though what she was going to say to him she had no idea.

*　　*　　*

Will was reading a journal at the kitchen table when Mallory walked in.

'Had a good morning?' he asked, looking up.

She relaxed. He was going to pretend nothing had happened. Good. She could do the same.

She suppressed the pang of disappointment before it had time to grab hold. What was there to be disappointed about? They didn't have a future.

'Two ear infections, two spotty viruses that weren't notifiable but will probably do the rounds of the kids in Darrowthwaite, a sebaceous cyst that needed excising...nothing really major,' she told him. 'Except my possible case of lupus. Obviously I'll have to wait for the blood test results but, from the symptoms she described, I'm pretty sure of the diagnosis. She mentioned having the butterfly rash.' Mallory frowned. 'Is there a lupus clinic at the local hospital, or am I going to have to send her further afield?'

'They set up a clinic a few months back,' Will said. He glanced at the carrier bags she was holding. 'Aren't you going climbing this afternoon?'

'With a cloudbase this low? It's no fun when you get to the top,' Mallory said. 'You can't see anything. You may as well be sitting on a rock on the ground as at the top of a mountain.'

'You're a fair-weather climber, then.'

'Better than not climbing at all.'

'Don't snipe.'

She flushed. 'Sorry. But you know how I feel about it.'

'And you know how *I* feel. So let's close the subject, hmm?'

'Just tell me. When you've had the day from hell, what do you do? Now you don't climb, that is.'

'Go to the gym, hammer the treadmill, swim a few

lengths. Maybe go rowing if it's decent weather for it. Why?'

'It's not the same, though, is it? You don't get the same rush as you do from climbing, the same endorphin high. And you don't get to save lives.'

'That,' Will said crisply, 'is *my* business.'

OK, maybe she'd gone too far. Time to back off. 'I got some French bread on the way home,' she said. 'It's still warm. Do you want cheese, ham or pâté with it?'

'Whatever comes to hand first.'

'Cheese,' she said, rummaging in the fridge. 'So how was your morning?'

'As exciting as it can be with a pinned leg and a cast.'

So *that* was what was wrong with him. It wasn't what had happened last night—he was simply going stir-crazy, stuck inside. She knew she'd be much worse in his position. 'Sounds like you need some fresh air.' And a change of scenery. 'Do you want to go for a drive this afternoon?'

'Thanks for the offer, but I think I'd better decline.'

She flushed. He had a point—after what had happened between them, maybe it wasn't a good idea to get too close.

And he hardly said a word to her during lunch, except to thank her for the trouble she'd taken. Politely and very coolly.

This was worse—far worse—than what had happened between her and Geoff. She switched the kettle on and cleared the table in silence. Will didn't bother making even polite conversation. The more time stretched out, the worse she felt.

'It's not going to work, is it?' she asked as she put a mug of coffee in front of him and sat down in the chair opposite his.

'What isn't?'

'Me staying here. Or working as your locum. Look, I know I said I'd stay until you were fit enough to work again, but in the circumstances…maybe you should start interviewing now for another locum. I'll leave as soon as you've found a replacement.'

'Mallory, you don't have to do that. I'm happy for you to stay as my locum—to stay here.'

'Well, you're certainly not acting as if you are.'

'Fair point.' Will sighed. 'I'm sorry. I'm behaving badly. I don't mean to take things out on you.'

'But it's frustrating, being stuck in one place, dependent on other people when you're used to fending for yourself.'

'Yeah.'

'And I've been nagging you.'

'Understatement.'

She sighed. 'I just want…to make things better.'

'Do you?'

His eyes were saying it all for him. *Kiss it better, then.*

She knew it was stupid. She knew it was crazy. But she did it anyway. She walked over to him, cupped his face between her hands and lowered her mouth to his.

He was the one to break it. 'No,' he said, his face tortured. 'We can't do this, Mallory. It's not sensible.'

'I know.' So why were her hands locked round his neck?

'We're not right for each other.'

'I know.' So why was he dropping those tiny butterfly kisses along her lower lip? Why was she tipping her head back to encourage him to deepen those kisses?

'It's not going to work out.'

'I know.' So why was she moving closer to him, burrowing her hands under his T-shirt to caress his warm, soft skin?

The first knock at the door Mallory assumed was merely the sound of her heart, her pulse was beating so hard and fast.

The second knock made them both pause.

And the third had them staring at each other.

'Someone's at the door,' Will said unnecessarily.

'I'll go,' Mallory said, sliding off his lap and raking her hands through her hair in an attempt to restore some sort of order to it.

'Hello, Mallory. Just dropped in to see Will,' Marion said.

'Um, come in,' Mallory mumbled, flushing bright pink. The practice receptionist never missed a thing. She was bound to realise what had been going on. 'The kettle's hot. I'll, um, make you a coffee.'

By the time Mallory led Marion through to the kitchen, Will had restored order to his clothes. But when she'd made her excuses and fled to the bathroom, Mallory saw for herself just how bad the situation had looked. Her face was flushed, her mouth was clearly swollen with kisses, her eyes were huge and dark and her hair was mussed. It was obvious to anyone what had been going on. And to someone as eagle-eyed as Marion Prentiss…

She had a nasty feeling she was in for a lecture. A big one.

CHAPTER THIRTEEN

MALLORY was right. Before she'd even seen her first patient the next morning, Marion rapped on her door. 'Thought you might like a cup of coffee,' she said.

'Thanks, Marion.' Mallory gave her a nervous smile. 'But I know you're busy. I can get my own coffee. I really don't expect you to wait on me.'

'No problem.' Marion paused. 'Actually, I wanted a word with you.'

Here it came.

'About Will. He's had a hard time of it.'

Mallory nodded. 'I know.'

'I don't just mean the accident. I mean before.'

'Roland.'

'He told you about that?' Marion was clearly surprised. 'I nagged him into it.'

'With that, and then Julie leaving to work abroad... He's been hurt. Badly.'

'He just needs to believe in himself again. To climb again,' Mallory said.

'Don't you think we've all tried to persuade him over the last five years? He used to be so laid-back and cheerful, always smiling. Nowadays all he does is work. He's good with his patients, never snaps at them, but he never really smiles, even at the little ones. I can't remember the last time I saw him smile properly.'

Mallory could. And the memory made her skin heat.

'He's driving himself into the ground. He won't listen to anyone—and he needs someone to stop him before it's too late.'

'And you think I'm that person?'

'No,' said Marion. 'I don't think it, Mallory. I *know* it.' She went back into brisk receptionist mode. 'I'll send your first patient in, shall I, Dr Ryman?'

'Thank you.'

Mallory took a swig of coffee as the receptionist left. Well, that was a turn-up for the books. There was one person in the world who thought she was right for Will.

Pity that person wasn't Will himself.

'Come in,' she called as she heard a diffident knock at the door.

Emma Wilson sat down in the chair Mallory offered her. 'I feel a bit silly, coming to you about this,' she said. 'But my husband insisted.' She bit her lip. 'I mean, pins and needles are quite normal, aren't they?'

'It depends,' Mallory said. 'Where do you get it, and how often?'

'In my hands. Most nights,' Emma said. 'I wake up sometimes and my left hand's gone numb.'

'Do you get it anywhere else?' Mallory asked.

Emma shook her head. 'Just my hands.'

'Any particular part?'

'My thumb and middle finger.'

There were two main possibilities, Mallory thought. 'Do you use a computer at all?'

'Once in a blue moon. If my husband's not on it, the kids are.' She smiled wryly. 'He said it might be RSI.'

'What do you do?' Mallory asked.

'I'm a florist.'

'So you need to do lots of little repeated movements?'

'Not really,' Emma said. 'Not like working on a machine or a computer.'

'It could be carpal tunnel syndrome,' Mallory said. 'Did you ever have it when you were pregnant?'

Emma frowned. 'It probably started around then. But…once you're pregnant, it goes away, doesn't it?'

'Not necessarily,' Mallory said. 'Sometimes you're unlucky and it stays with you.' Particularly if you were overweight, as Emma was. 'Do you find it gets better if you hang your hand over the edge of the bed or shake it?'

Emma nodded.

'That's fairly common.' Mallory stretched out her wrist. 'You've got nine tendons and a nerve called the median nerve, all competing for space within the wrist. The median nerve passes through a gap under a ligament at the front of the wrist, called the carpal tunnel—and it gets compressed, particularly in pregnancy. When that happens, you end up with numbness, tingling and pain in your thumb, index and middle fingers. I'd like to try a couple of tests, if I may?'

'Of course.'

'I'd like you to flex your wrist for me, as much as you can.'

Emma did so, and Mallory watched the second hand on the clock sweep all the way round. The action—known as Phalen's test—sometimes caused tingling and pins and needles in patients who had carpal tunnel syndrome.

'Anything feel different?' Mallory asked.

'Just aches a bit.'

Well, the test wasn't always reliable. Next, Mallory tried Tinel's test, tapping the nerve over the wrist. 'How about now?'

'It tingles a bit,' Emma said. 'Not as bad as at night.'

Mallory nodded. 'I think it's carpal tunnel syndrome. You might find that losing a few pounds helps—it'll take some of the pressure off your wrists.'

Emma grimaced. 'I've been on more diets than you've had hot dinners. Can't stick to them.'

'Think of it as healthy eating rather than depriving yourself,' Mallory advised. 'And you don't have to do it all by diet. If you eat just two hundred and fifty calories less than you need each day and do two hundred and fifty calories' worth of exercise too, you'll lose a steady pound a week.'

'Well, there's no harm in trying,' Emma said, not sounding convinced.

'Just little changes can make a difference,' Mallory said. 'If you make a sandwich, don't put butter on the bread first. Switch to skimmed milk. Swap sugared breakfast cereals for wholegrain cereals without sugar—mix them together and gradually decrease the proportion of sugared cereals.' She smiled. 'I know sometimes it's hard to motivate yourself to diet.'

'You don't look as if you've ever needed to diet,' Emma said wryly.

'No. I've been lucky with my genes—plus, I climb at weekends.'

Emma looked horrified. 'I don't think I want to do climbing!'

'You don't have to. Try swimming—that's great for you. And walking.'

'I'll give it a try,' Emma promised.

'To help your wrists, you can also take a couple of ibuprofen before you go to bed—anti-inflammatories sometimes help take a lot of the pressure off the nerve. If that doesn't work, we can try a splint or a cortisone injection. If we do an injection, you might find the pain's a lot worse for a couple of days and then improves dramatically. And if that fails, we can relieve the compression by cutting the ligament. It's a fairly quick procedure and we can do it here—you won't have to go to hospital.'

'Surgery?' Emma's eyes grew round.

Clearly another patient who was terrified by the idea of a knife. Probably by the thought of the steroid injection, too. 'Hopefully it won't come to that. We'll try the anti-inflammatories first.' Mallory smiled. 'Yoga can help, too—there was a study a couple of years back that showed women who used the *namaste* or prayer position in yoga had to flex their wrists a bit more, and this helped to the point where they didn't need surgery for carpal tunnel syndrome.'

'I might try that. I read something about rebound headaches if you kept taking painkillers,' Emma said.

'That can happen if you overuse painkillers, but you shouldn't have any problems,' Mallory reassured her, 'not with just a couple of ibuprofen last thing at night. Give it a couple of weeks. If you're still having problems, come back and see me and we'll try a splint.'

'Thank you, Dr Ryman. I hope I haven't, well, wasted your time. You know, time another patient needed.'

'Not at all. You've had a health problem so you've got as much right as anyone else to see me about it. And I hope I've put your mind at rest.'

'You have. Thanks.'

Mallory smiled as Emma left the consulting room, updated the notes, then buzzed Marion to say that she was ready for her next patient. Everything was ticking over as normal.

Except the fact that she couldn't get Will Cooper out of her head.

Will and Mallory spent the next few days pussyfooting around each other and pretending that neither of them thought a thing about the love-making they'd shared. The kisses. The touching. Both of them took to reading journals and giving the other surreptitious glances when they thought they weren't looking.

And then Will had an unexpected visitor.

'You look terrible,' Anne Cooper informed her son as she closed the kitchen door behind her. 'Where's this doctor who's supposed to be looking after you?'

'At the surgery, taking my list,' Will answered crisply.

'Hmm. I'll make us some coffee.' Anne checked out the fridge in the seconds it took her to retrieve the milk. 'Doesn't believe in square meals, does she?' she asked.

'I haven't asked her to cook for me.'

'Well, *you* can't do it, can you?' Anne raised an eyebrow. 'So what are you doing? Living on sandwiches?'

'Take-aways mainly. And it isn't a problem, Mum. Don't try to make it into one.'

Anne narrowed her eyes. 'Are you accusing me of interfering?'

'No.'

'Good. Because you don't let me close enough to interfere.' Her mouth tightened. 'I would have come to look after you. Or you could have come home. You know that.'

He shook his head. 'Thanks, but we've already been through that. We'd drive each other mad. I've got my ways, you've got yours, and they're not the same. Anyway, you're busy.' Retirement hadn't suited his mother. She'd become a magistrate, so she could still spend most of her time in the legal world she'd loved.

'Hmm.' Anne finished making coffee and poured a mug out for Will. 'I still have enough time to worry about you, Will,' she said. 'I hate the way you've closed yourself off since Roly died.'

'Mum, leave it.'

'No, Will, I've tried leaving you alone and it hasn't made you come to terms with what happened.'

'I'm not one of your legal cases.'

'I know you're not. They're a hell of a lot easier to sort out.'

He stared at her in surprise.

'Maybe I haven't told you this often enough. You're my son, I'm proud of you, and I love you. And you're driving yourself into the ground. Work isn't everything.'

He laughed. 'That's rich, coming from you. The woman who lasted three months into retirement, then went straight back to work.'

She allowed herself a smile. 'All right. Pots and kettles.'

'Exactly. So stop nagging, Mummy, dearest.' He looked at her. 'So what's the real reason for your visit?'

'Julie.'

He forced himself not to flinch. 'Julie.'

'I promised her I wouldn't tell you, but...' Anne sighed. 'Look, I know everything that happened that night.'

Ice trickled down his spine. 'I don't know what you mean.'

'She told me about Roly. How she'd fallen in love with him, left you.' Anne bit her lip. 'I should have guessed your brother had pulled some kind of stunt. He always did want everything you had, with sugar on it. And close your mouth, Will. I'm not stupid.'

'But I thought...'

'You thought he pulled the wool over my eyes. No. Generally it was easier to go along with him than make a scene and then have him do something even worse. Oh, don't think I didn't love him. I did. I *do*. I still miss him. But I know what he could be like.'

'I never realised.'

'You weren't meant to,' Anne said dryly.

'So why today? Why are you telling me now?'

'Because I've had a letter from Julie. She's not working for Médicins Sans Frontières any more—she's in Australia, working as the nurse at a GP practice in the outback. And she's married to one of the partners.'

Will took a swig of coffee. 'Don't try to sugar the pill, will you, Mum?'

'I've tried the softly-softly approach with you. It doesn't work. So now I'm telling you straight. I know you loved her, and maybe you always hoped she'd come back to you. But it's not going to happen, Will. She's married.'

The news should hurt.

But Will didn't feel anything. No pain, not even a twinge of regret for long-splintered plans that would never be glued together again. 'I hope she's happy.' To his surprise, he meant it.

'She sounds it. She told me that she'd never forget Roly—or you—but she'd made some kind of sense of her life now.'

'Good.'

'And now it's time for you to move on, too. Really move on. If you don't want to go back to climbing, fair enough— but you don't need to punish yourself any more. Because it was never your fault, what happened to your brother. If anything, it was probably his—the chances were he didn't check his equipment properly.'

'Because he felt guilty about what he'd done to me, you mean?' It had never occurred to Will before that Roly might have done it deliberately.

'No. Because that was the way he was. Devil-may-care. You know that as well as I do.'

There was nothing Will could say to that.

'Mallory sounds nice.'

This time, he did react. 'Have you got spies trained on me or something?'

'How else am I supposed to keep track of what you're doing if you won't tell me yourself?'

'It's an invasion of privacy.'

'It's called parenthood. Caring,' she said crisply. 'And, no, I'm not going to tell you who keeps an eye on you for me.'

Will could have named a few suspects, but chose not to. 'Don't get any ideas. She's my locum.'

'Yes, dear.'

He had a sudden vision of Mallory ganging up with his mother. And a two-year-old running rings round them both. A two-year-old climbing on her grandmother's knee demanding a story. A two-year-old with blue eyes and fine auburn hair—a two-year-old who'd virtually been born with an ice pick in her hand and was already shinning up toddler gym equipment with ease. A two-year-old just like her mother…

Hell. He must have it bad if he was dreaming about having children with Mallory.

Anne spread her hands. 'Just think about it.'

Will flushed. It would be just his luck that his mother had second sight and knew exactly what he'd just been daydreaming about. 'You're impossible.'

'Like mother, like son,' she riposted. 'And I'd rather like my son back. I've been missing you for quite a while, Will.'

'I'm fine, Mum.'

'Nobody else thinks so.' She ruffled his hair. 'But you're disgustingly stubborn.'

'Wonder where I get that from?' he muttered.

She chuckled. 'Pots and kettles,' she said again. 'Look, I'm due in court in half an hour.'

Now, there was a surprise, Will thought.

'But I brought you some cake.'

'Home-made by Darrowthwaite Bakery,' he guessed dryly.

'In my day,' she said, 'women had to fight tooth and nail to get a decent career—that's if they ever managed to get through the glass ceiling. And woe betide them if they didn't have a clean house, cooked every single family meal themselves, have a perfectly manicured garden or offer six different sorts of home-made cake to any stray guest. Not to mention bringing up the children without any sort of domestic support.' She shrugged. 'Something had to give. I chose cooking.'

Yeah. He knew someone else who thought like that. This time Will's smile was genuine. 'You still managed to be Supermum, though. You always made it to assembly and the school play and parents' evenings.'

'Well, of course I did.' Anne smiled back. 'And I'm quite prepared to make an exception to my rule and bake you as many cakes as you like, if it means I get my gorgeous son back.'

'Is that a challenge, Mum?'

'No. It's a fact.'

'I just need some time.'

'You've had plenty of time,' Anne pointed out. 'I've given you space. Too much space, I think. So now I'm telling you, son. What you need is to stop brooding, stop blaming yourself and start living again. Go and have some fun.'

'I'm the serious twin, remember?'

'You can be serious and still have fun. And don't tell me you were a goody two-shoes at med school either. I know who drew that cartoon of Professor Macreadie and plastered copies around the medical block after your finals.'

'Is there anything you *don't* know?' Will asked, amused despite his annoyance.

Anne simply smiled. 'Tell me, when you're a parent.'

'I thought I might have eaten something that disagreed with me,' Zoe said.

'Any diarrhoea? Sickness?' Mallory asked.

'Nothing. Though it hurts when I have a wee.'

Mallory went on red alert. 'Where exactly does it hurt?' she asked.

'On this side.' Zoe pointed to the lower right-hand side of her abdomen.

Mallory mentally listed the possible causes of pain in that area. The appendix; a problem in the caecum—the widest part of the large intestine; a stone in the ureter, the tube carrying urine from the kidney to the bladder; or maybe a problem in the Fallopian tube or ovary.

She pushed back the thought of Lindy. That wasn't going to happen again. She wasn't going to make the same mistake. And she wasn't going to overcompensate either. She'd proved to herself in the time she'd acted as Will's locum that she could still be a competent doctor. So she ignored the hot feeling at the back of her neck. Or, rather, tried to. 'Do you mind if I examine you?' she asked.

Zoe nodded and bared her abdomen.

Mallory examined her gently.

'Ow, that hurts,' Zoe said.

No rebound pain from the other side—but there was some guarding of the abdomen, Mallory noticed. 'Any chance you could be pregnant?' she asked.

'I hope not! We're always careful,' Zoe said.

'When was your last period?'

'About four or five weeks ago. I've never been that regular.'

'Are you having a period now?'

'No.'

'Any pain in your shoulder?'

'No.'

Maybe she was just being paranoid. Overcompensating for what had happened with Lindy. But... 'I'm sending you to hospital,' she said quietly. 'I think you might have an ectopic pregnancy—that's where the embryo has implanted in your Fallopian tube instead of your womb. I'd like them to give you an ultrasound to check what's going on.'

'What happens if I do have an ectopic pregnancy?'

'The surgeon will do a laparoscopy—that's where he'll make a tiny cut in your abdomen and put a camera inside you so he can see what he's doing. He'll remove the embryo and repair your Fallopian tube.'

'And I'll still be able to have a baby in a few years?'

'You should be able to. Though there's a higher risk of having an ectopic pregnancy in the future, so you'll have an early scan to check all's well,' Mallory explained. 'I'm going to call the hospital now, so they'll be expecting you. And I'll write a letter for you to take in with you.'

By the time Mallory returned to the cottage, she felt totally drained.

'Are you OK?' Will asked.

'Yeah. Just laying a few ghosts to rest, I guess.'

His eyes narrowed. 'Meaning?'

'I've just had a suspected ectopic. I might be wrong—but I've sent her to hospital. No bleeding, no shoulder pain—but she was guarding, and it's four or five weeks since her last period, though she told me she was irregular.'

'Better to be on the safe side,' Will said.

Which they definitely weren't. With each other, at least.

'I brought us some bagels for lunch,' she told him. 'Smoked salmon and dill mayonnaise OK with you?'

'Sounds perfect. And chocolate cake for pudding.'

'No cake.'

He nodded at the bag on the worktop. 'Oh, yes, there is.'

'Another concerned patient wanting to know when you'll be back so they can get rid of your terrible locum?' she teased.

'My mother, actually.'

'Your mother.' Will had barely mentioned his parents in the weeks she'd been there. Knowing Will as she did, Mallory suspected that Will kept his family very much at arm's length.

'She'd had some news about Julie.'

Mallory went very still. Julie. Will's ex-fiancée. The

woman that he was still in love with, even though he wasn't admitting it. 'What about her?'

'She's moved to Australia. Married to a GP.'

And Will's mother had just knocked the bottom straight out of his world by telling him. 'I'm sorry,' she said softly.

Her first instinct was to put her arms round him. She stopped herself. Just. Because she knew exactly where it would lead if she did.

'Julie's been out of reach for a long, long time,' Will said. 'She flew out straight after Roly's funeral to join Médicins Sans Frontières. I thought at the time she was running away—I even told her that. Not that she listened. And she was right. It was what she needed. She's found what she wants in life now.' He looked levelly at her. 'You're very like her.'

Meaning what? That she was a substitute—that during their love-making, he'd seen Julie rather than her? Or was he telling her that he'd made that mistake once and never would again? 'I'm not sure how to take that.'

'Face value,' Will told her. 'You're both free spirits, both climbers, both considered working in extreme conditions.'

There was no answer to that. Mallory busied herself putting their lunch onto plates. 'Your mother couldn't stay for lunch, then?'

'No. She was due in court,' he said. 'You all right after this morning? Your suspected ectopic?'

She nodded.

'One demon less to face.' He toyed with the bagel she placed in front of him. 'So, have you made a decision about your career yet?'

'Sort of. I'm going to stay in medicine,' she said. 'Working here's taught me that it's what I want to do. I'm not just trying to please Dad.'

'Are you still thinking about extreme conditions training or joining Médicins Sans Frontières?'

Mallory shrugged. 'Possibly. Depends if I can find another GP post.'

'*If.* You're kidding, right?' He rolled his eyes. 'You know there's a shortage of GPs.'

'Yes. What I meant was find a post that suits me.'

'Well, you don't have to worry about references. Charles gave you an excellent one. We'll do the same.'

The way he was talking, it was obvious Will could hardly wait to get back to work. And for her to leave.

As for the secret hopes she'd cherished that maybe he'd miss her and ask her to stay—hopes so secret that she'd barely admitted them to herself—they withered within seconds. No, when she left here, that would be the last she ever saw of Will Cooper. And there was no point in being upset about it. Because he'd retreated back into self-containment. He clearly didn't want her in his life. She'd be too much of a complication.

If she had any sense, she'd take the same approach.

CHAPTER FOURTEEN

LATER that afternoon, Will looked up from the medical journal he'd been studying. 'Just ring the hospital, Mallory.'

'What?'

'You're not going to rest until you know about your patient. Ring the hospital.'

She knew he was right. But still her hand hesitated over the receiver. Had she made the right judgement call this time?

'Mallory, I'd offer to do it for you, but this is something you need to do yourself,' he said, quite gently.

'I know.' But her fingers were still shaking as she keyed in the hospital's number—enough so that she misdialled twice. But at last she was through. And at last she got the answer.

'It was an ectopic,' she told Will when she'd replaced the receiver. 'But they caught her early enough to repair her Fallopian tube.'

'Good.' He picked up his crutches and manoeuvred himself over to her so he could place a comforting hand on her shoulder. 'So now you can lay your demons to rest. You're a perfectly competent GP—and you know it.'

Maybe it was the fact that his touch made her knees go weak that turned her tongue to acid. 'Yes, I've faced my demons. Isn't it time you faced yours?'

He removed his hand as if she'd stung him. 'I don't have any demons,' he informed her stiffly. 'I'm perfectly fine.'

She didn't believe him. But she'd lost her taste for arguing. She simply said, 'Good,' and left the room before she said something they'd both regret.

Three days of being carefully polite to Will—three days in which it hadn't been good enough weather for her to go climbing, and the local climbing wall wasn't enough of a challenge to keep her satisfied—had driven Mallory to breaking point.

And then her mobile phone shrilled. She glanced at the display before answering it: *DMR Base*. It looked like another call-out. 'Hello, Mallory Ryman speaking.'

'Mallory, it's Rob Viner. We've a full-scale search on, including rescue dogs. Can you meet us here at the base?' he asked.

'I'm on my way. What do we know so far?'

'Our missing person's Edward Becker—Eddie—aged fifteen. He skipped school today and it was only when he didn't come home that his mother raised the alarm. One of his mates said he'd been planning to go climbing but wasn't sure where—he thinks it might be Skiddaw. Eddie's mobile phone is switched off and his mother's going frantic.'

Eddie. Mallory knew that name. Edward Becker. She searched her memory. 'Not Cathy's son, by any chance?'

'Yes. You know him?'

'No, but he's on our patient list. I'll check with Will in case there's anything we should know. I'll bring my kit with me.'

'Cheers.' Rob rang off.

Mallory went through to the living room. 'Will, I've been called out on a search. I'm off to the MR team base now.'

'OK.'

'Anything you need before I go?'

Will shook his head.

'Good.' She paused. 'He's one of our patients. I won-

dered if there was anything I should know about him med-
ically—Edward Becker?'

'Cathy's boy?' Will frowned. 'No, Eddie doesn't have
any medical conditions. But Cathy must be going frantic.'

'Yeah. And we still haven't managed to help her with
Frank. Let's just hope this isn't the proverbial straw to
break her back,' Mallory said.

'I'll ring her and tell her you've joined the search if you
like. And the minute you hear anything…'

'I'll keep in touch,' she promised.

'Just be careful, OK?'

'Yeah.' She took a deep breath, grabbed her doctor's bag
and climbing kit, and headed out to the base.

'He's been skipping school for weeks,' Cathy sobbed. 'It's
all my fault. I should have noticed he wasn't himself—I
was so preoccupied with Dad. What if he's hurt himself
really badly? What if he's fallen somewhere and been
killed?'

'Darrowthwaite Mountain Rescue team will find him,'
Will said soothingly. 'They started the search as soon as
you told them he was missing, gone climbing. Mallory's
out there with them.'

'Oh, God, why didn't I notice?' Cathy wailed.

'You've had a lot on your plate. More than a lot,' Will
said. 'You're not to blame.'

'If he's dead…'

Yeah. Will knew all about that. 'They're all doing what
they can,' he said softly. 'They'll find him.'

'A couple at one of the bed and breakfast places rang in
and said they saw a boy climbing on his own a couple of
hours ago,' Rob said. 'So we're concentrating in the area
where they saw him.'

'Right.' Mallory walked along beside him, scanning the

area. The light was already fading. If they didn't find him soon, they had a real potential problem. It'd be too dark to see what they were doing—and the temperature was dropping. If Eddie had fallen, he could be lying on exposed rock. The chances were he'd end up with hypothermia—and that was looking on the bright side. Add blood loss, concussion, the potential for slipping and falling even further, resulting in multiple fractures and internal injuries...

Almost as if he'd read her mind, Rob said, 'Let's just hope this is a false alarm—that he's holed up somewhere safe and warm.'

'But you don't think so.'

Rob shook his head. 'He's been climbing since he was about ten. Started off on the climbing wall at the adventure centre and moved up from there—he's been training with us for months. But he stopped coming a month or so before Christmas.' He sighed. 'I wish I'd pushed a bit harder, gone to see the kid and asked him what was wrong. He wasn't the type to just get bored and drop out. Eddie was always a nice kid.'

'But there was always something else that needed doing more urgently and you never got round to it, and then it seemed as if you were making a fuss because you'd left it too long and anyway he was a teenager, so maybe he'd just grown out of wanting to do rescue work,' Mallory said. 'Don't try to be wise with hindsight, Rob. You're doing yourself an injustice.'

'Are there any medical conditions we need to know about?'

'No. So hopefully he's either safe and warm somewhere or he's just got stuck and we'll find him,' Mallory said.

'Yeah.'

'Concentrate on the now, not the might-have-beens.'

He chuckled. 'For someone so small, you're incredibly bossy.'

'All part of doctor training,' she teased back. 'Come on. Let's find young Eddie. Are you going first, or am I?'

Will thought he could handle staying in the cottage on his own. Hadn't he told himself that he wasn't involved with Mallory, that she could leave in a couple of weeks and he'd be fine about it?

And yet he found himself pacing the room. Laboriously. On crutches. And it wasn't enough to keep his mind occupied.

He knew he should keep the line free, just in case, but... Unable to help himself, he rang the base. 'Any news yet?' he asked when Laura Mercer answered.

'They're still looking.'

'Hell.' Will knew from experience that the longer the team had to search, the worse condition the patient was likely to be in. Mallory might well need back-up medical advice. She couldn't waste time trying to ring him here— she might not even be *able* to ring him if she was in a dead area for mobile phone signals. And he didn't have radio contact here. So he had to be there, at the base, for when she needed him.

The place he'd sworn he'd never, ever set foot in again.

Maybe Mallory was right. Maybe it *was* time to face his demons. 'Laura,' he said softly, 'I'm getting a taxi. I'll be with you as soon as I can.'

After two hours of searching—when they were all cold, tired and on edge—Rob's radio crackled into life. 'Search dog Rusty's found Eddie.'

Rusty. Will's old dog. Mallory felt tears pricking her eyes.

'Is he conscious?' Rob asked.

'Not sure. He's fallen and landed on a ledge—we don't

know how far or what his injuries are. Euan says it's minus one out there, so he might have hypothermia.'

'Where is he?'

Laura gave them a grid reference. 'We're going to send a stretcher down for him.'

Mallory, who'd heard every word, nudged Rob. 'We're near enough. By the time they've put the anchors in we can be there. I'll go down—as a doctor, I'm in a better position to check his injuries. But I think we ought to call the air rescue in. If he's in a bad way, it's going to take too long for the ambulance to get him to hospital.'

Rob nodded. 'OK. Let's go.'

'What's happening?' Will asked as he manoeuvred his crutches into the radio control room.

'They've found Eddie Becker on Skiddaw. Mallory's going down with a stretcher and we're calling the air ambulance in,' Laura explained.

Mallory was going down with a stretcher. The air temperature was low enough to make the rocks slippery and dangerous. Hell. If only he wasn't on crutches, he could have been there, too. Doing the stretcher bit instead of her, to make sure she stayed safe.

The fact that he hadn't climbed in five years was completely irrelevant.

'OK. Have you phoned Cathy yet, or do you want me to do it?'

'Would you?' Laura gave him a grateful look.

He should have been the one giving *her* a grateful look. At least now he had something to do, instead of waiting and worrying. 'Sure.' Will took his mobile phone from his pocket and tapped in Cathy's number.

'Hey, there.' Mallory crouched on the narrow ledge next to Eddie. Moisture from the air had settled on the rocks; it was just below freezing and the surface was extremely slippery. She'd picked her way carefully down five metres of scree so no loose stones had fallen and injured Eddie further, and there was another ten metres or so of scree beneath them. If she wasn't careful, both she and Eddie would end up sliding down it. 'Eddie?'

'Yeah.' The boy's voice was faint and hoarse.

'I'm Mallory Ryman. I'm a doctor with the mountain rescue team. How are you feeling?'

'Head hurts.'

He wasn't complaining of cold: that was a bad sign. When hypothermia had set in, the shiver mechanism, which worked to generate warmth and protect the body, was overwhelmed by heat loss, and sufferers of hypothermia reached a point where they couldn't recognise that they were cold—some even removed their clothing, saying they were hot. 'OK.' The light attached to Mallory's climbing helmet really wasn't good enough for her to give him a proper examination—she'd just have to do the best she could. 'How long have you been here?'

'Dunno.'

He sounded drowsy and her light showed that he looked pale and puffy-faced. His breathing was slow, as was his pulse, but his body hadn't shut down completely. She needed to get him warm. A cardiac arrest on the side of a mountain, in the dark and with no portable shocking equipment to help her, would be a nightmare. 'You're suffering from hypothermia. I've got a space blanket,' Mallory said, 'and I'm going to put it round you. But first I need to check any other damage.'

There were several lacerations to his face for a start. But at least his pupils were equal.

'What happened to your helmet?' she asked.

'Didn't need one.'

'Whistle?' From what Rob had told her, Eddie knew

enough about rescue work and fell-walking to know the international distress signal—six blasts on a whistle, repeated at one-minute intervals. And he knew well enough to carry a whistle as well as a helmet.

'Rob tells me you're an experienced climber.'

Eddie scowled.

She decided not to press the point. 'Where else does it hurt?'

'Ankle.'

She examined him gently. His gasp of pain told her it was tender, and she could feel swelling in the area, indicating that he'd broken it. 'Anywhere else?'

'No.'

Though that wasn't necessarily a good sign. His nervous system was too cold to function properly—he could have internal injuries which he wasn't feeling.

Gently, she checked both arms. There was swelling around one wrist, as if he'd banged it hard when he'd fallen. He wasn't feeling that either.

'Do you know how far you fell?'

'Dunno.'

'Did you black out?'

'Dunno.'

Don't know or don't want to say? she wondered. 'OK. If you're not sure, we'll assume that you lost consciousness, to be on the safe side.' She radioed up to Rob, 'Get a CT scan organised at the hospital. Possible loss of consciousness. Fractured right ankle, possible Colles' fracture right wrist, moderate hypothermia.'

'OK, Mallory. Received and out.'

'What's it to you, anyway?' Eddie muttered.

'You're my patient. I'm a doctor. It's my job.'

'Yeah, well, don't matter.'

'What doesn't matter?' she asked.

He gave her another sullen look.

'Eddie, I know you used to work with the MR team. And you stopped going before Christmas. Did something happen?'

'Nothing anyone can do.'

'Try me,' Mallory said.

'It's like they say at school. My grandad's mental and I'll go the same way. So there's no point in joining the rescue team 'cos they'll kick me out when they find out about my grandad.'

So that was it. He'd been teased. Badly, from the sound of it.

'And they're right. Mum's going like he is.'

'You think your mother's got the same problem as your grandfather?'

''S obvious.'

'Your mum's just had a tough time of it lately. Sounds as if you have, too.' Mallory paused. 'And it's not true. What your grandfather has…it's not contagious and it doesn't necessarily run in families.'

Eddie was silent.

'Eddie? You still with me?'

'Yeah,' he mumbled.

Though this time it sounded more like a teenager's 'I don't want to talk' than a physical inability to answer brought on by worsening hypothermia.

'Your mum's been really worried about you, you know,' Mallory added.

'Yeah, *right.*' Said with all the scorn he could muster.

Mallory remembered what Cathy had said during her consultation. *Doing it for attention… They'll leave home the minute they're sixteen…* Clearly Cathy wasn't the only one suffering from the effects of her father's illness. 'I know,' she said carefully, 'things have been really tough at home lately. But it doesn't mean your mum doesn't love you.'

'No, she doesn't. Since Grandad came to live with us, he's all she thinks about. If she's not running round after him enough, he makes out he's ill.'

'He can't help it,' Mallory said.

'Yes, he can. Sometimes I really hate him—the way he's spoiled things. Everything was all right at home until he came. That's why I come up here, to get away from him and his moaning.'

Mallory gently put a collar round his neck to immobilise his spine. 'Climbing's good when you're down. It gives you something else to think about.'

He looked at her in surprise. 'You're not going to say I shouldn't have done it?'

'Nope. I do it myself. Though next time it might be an idea to come a bit better prepared. Tell someone where you're going or at least leave a few route cards on your way, bring warm clothes and something to eat and drink. Not forgetting the whistle and your mobile phone. So then if you do have an accident, we can find you a lot quicker.'

'My phone's battery ran out,' he said. 'I didn't mean to make Mum worry. It's just…I'm sick of Grandad being there all the time. She never has time for me and my sister any more. Or Dad.'

'Maybe I can do something to help,' she said gently. 'Something to make him better, so you'll enjoy his company.'

'Pigs might fly. You'll never stop him moaning.' He paused. 'Do you really go climbing when you're miserable?'

'Yep. When I've got a problem, I head for the hills. That way I have to concentrate on something else, and by the time I've got to the top my subconscious has been ticking away and I've got more idea of how to fix what's wrong.'

'And it always works?'

'Mostly.'

'And you go climbing on your own?'

'I did, last weekend,' she said.

'Why?'

There was no harm in telling him, Mallory reasoned. It might take his mind off the pain as she eased him onto the stretcher and wrapped the space blanket round him.

'Someone I met. Someone I think could be very special to me—but I don't think he feels the same way about me. So maybe it's better that I leave.'

Will froze as her words crackled through the radio. Did Mallory realise she was still transmitting? Was this her way of telling him how she felt about him?

No. Of course not. She didn't even know he was in the control room.

Was she talking about him? Someone who could be special to her... It could be Geoff. Maybe she'd realised she was making a huge mistake, that Geoff was the one for her.

But she'd also talked about 'someone who didn't feel the same way about her'. She already knew Geoff loved her, to the point of asking her to marry him.

So maybe she *was* talking about *him*.

'Why don't you ask him if he wants you to stay?' Eddie asked.

'Because,' Mallory said quietly, 'I'm scared he might say no.' The sound of rotors above her told her that the helicopter had arrived. 'We're going to airlift you to hospital, Eddie. Get you warmed up, fix the broken bones, check you haven't done any other damage—I'd do it myself, only there aren't any X-ray machines on Skiddaw.'

'Nah.' He smiled at her poor joke.

'Ready when you are,' she said into the radio.

'Line's on its way down with a winch man,' Rob told her.

'OK. We're here and waiting,' Mallory said.

Eddie squeezed her hand. 'Thank you. For rescuing me.'

'Hey, no problem. Just don't do it again.' She winked at him. 'And I'll try to do something about your other problem. That's just between you and me, OK?'

Eddie was shortly being winched into the helicopter. But on the way up the stretcher was caught by a gust of wind and banged against the rocks. Loose scree began to bounce down towards the narrow ledge where Mallory was standing. Although she tried to flatten herself against the face of the cliff, it wasn't enough to protect her. A large rock slammed into her helmet. Just as everything went black, she heard herself calling his name. 'Will…'

CHAPTER FIFTEEN

'MALLORY? Come in, Mallory,' Will said, trying to keep the panic from his voice.

The radio hissed back.

'Base to Ryman. Mallory, are you all right?'

Still nothing.

He switched frequency to Rob Viner's radio. 'Rob, it's Will. What's happening?'

'Will? But…what are you doing at the base?'

'I'll explain later. Mallory's not answering her radio. What's happening?' he repeated.

'The stretcher knocked some scree loose—I think it must have hit her. I'm going down to her now.'

Will had to know. 'Is she still in a harness?'

'She climbs by the book, Will. Just like you did.'

'OK. Radio in when you're down there with her.'

'Do you want me to take over?' Laura asked.

'No. I'll stay in touch with Rob. You cover the hospitals,' Will directed. 'Is an ambulance on its way to Skiddaw?'

'The one we called out the first time—it's on its way back, but it's the nearest,' Laura said. 'Unless Rob thinks she needs the air ambulance when he gets down there.'

Will worked out how long it would take the crew to airlift Eddie to Carlisle and get back to Skiddaw. Too long. The road ambulance was their best option. Provided Mallory hadn't been really badly injured… He forced himself not to think about that. He was a professional. He'd done this for years. Well, not recently but he knew the routine. 'OK. Can you ring Cathy Becker to let her know what's going on? I know I said I'd do it—'

'But Mallory's more important to you, right now,' Laura finished. 'OK, Dr Cooper.'

'It's Will,' he said, giving her a half-smile, then turned back to the radio. 'Rob. Are you with her yet?'

'Yes.'

'Conscious?'

'GCS 12, before you ask.'

Will smiled. The old rapport was still there. 'Good. Status report?'

'Both pupils equal and reacting. A few bruises, some lacerations. Her helmet's in a bad state—she's taken quite a knock.'

'Any guarding? Possible fractures? Internal injuries?'

'No, she's been lucky. We're going to stretcher her up and wait for the ambulance.'

'Good. No liquids,' Will warned. 'Even if she asks for it. Though put a space blanket round her. We don't want her getting hypothermia.'

'Roger. Get the hospital prepped for—'

'A CT scan,' Will finished.

'Yeah. Hey, Will?'

'Yes?'

'Welcome back,' Rob said softly.

Welcome back. It suddenly hit Will what he was doing. Sitting in the communications room as if he'd never been away, working as part of the team, giving calm and clear instructions over the phone.

Instructions about the woman he loved.

He swallowed the lump in his throat. 'Be careful with her, Rob.'

'I'll treat her like spun glass,' Rob promised. 'Do you want to talk to her?'

Yes. Of course he did. But he didn't want to delay her recovery. 'Just get her out of there, Rob.'

'OK, boss.'

By the time Mallory's stretcher was at the top, the ambulance was there and Will didn't get a chance to talk to her before she was in the vehicle and on her way to hospital.

He looked at Laura. 'I'm sorry. I barged in and took over without so much as a by your leave.'

'Hey, that's OK. I think the team's just glad to have you back,' Laura said. 'You *are* back, aren't you?'

He gave a rueful smile. 'Looks like it. I can't stay for the debriefing, though. I need to go to the hospital.' A phone call definitely wasn't good enough to tell him how Mallory *really* was. He needed to be there and see the situation for himself. 'Tell the team…tell them from me I'll shout them all a drink and a fish supper tomorrow night, OK?'

She nodded. 'Give Mallory our love.'

'Yeah.' And his own. If she'd have it.

Bright lights. Noise. But…wasn't she halfway down a mountain? Wasn't it supposed to be cold and windy and… Hypothermia? That was it. She'd been knocked out by a falling rock and lain there on Skiddaw all night. She had hypothermia. She was hallucinating. Because Will Cooper sure as hell wasn't halfway down a mountain with her. And right now she could see him sitting by her side.

'Welcome back to the land of the living,' he said softly.

'Huh?' Mallory blinked.

'You gave us all a scare.'

'That's my line.' She tried to focus and gave up. 'Wanna go to sleep.'

'Not until they've done your obs. I'd do them myself,

except…' he indicated his cast '…I have this small problem with writing and handling instruments.'

'How'd you get here?' she demanded. 'You can't drive!'

'Taxi. Though, believe me, I'd have walked here if I'd had to. And hopped when my crutches gave out.'

'I'm supposed to be looking after *you*.'

'Not when you're concussed. You're still on fifteen-minute obs, even though your CT scan was clear.'

So there wasn't an intracranial haematoma—a blood clot from a ruptured vessel in her brain. But she ached all over, and just about all the skin she could see was beginning to bruise. She tried to smile. 'Getting your own back?'

'I don't think anyone or anything could stop you doing what you wanted, Dr Ryman.' Will paused. 'Can you remember what happened?'

'Yes. We were winching Eddie out. The stretcher must've hit some loose rocks, which hit me.' She thought for a moment. 'Rob brought me back up.'

'Good. No memory loss, then.' Meaning that it was less likely she had a serious head injury—the severity of the injury was usually matched by the amount of memory loss before and after the trauma. His fingers tangled with hers. 'You scared the hell out of me when you didn't answer the radio.'

'Huh?' No. Her brain definitely wasn't focusing. She'd left him safely in the cottage. He hadn't been on Skiddaw… No, he couldn't have been. Not with crutches and a cast.

'The radio. You know, the thing you carry with you to stay in touch with the rest of the team and the base?'

'But…'

Will took pity on her. 'I was in the radio control room at the base.'

'You were *what*?'

'You heard. You see, there's this woman who's been nagging me. Telling me how selfish I am, how I should be out there still saving lives. And today, when I knew she was searching for someone who could be seriously hurt and she might need medical back-up, a second opinion…I couldn't stay sulking at home.'

'You went to the base.'

'Yes.'

'For me.'

'Yes and no.'

'But…'

'You were right,' he said softly. 'It was more than time I faced my demons. And now I have.'

'And?'

He nodded. 'I'm back on the team. On radio work for the time being—but as soon as my leg's right, I'll be buying a new pair of climbing boots and I'll be back in training.'

'That's good.'

'But there's a condition.'

Mallory frowned. 'What's that?'

'I want to do it in a partnership.'

'I don't follow.'

'What you told Eddie,' he said softly. 'Did you mean it?'

'Mean what?'

'That you've met someone special. But you're scared to ask him if he wants you to stay because you think he'll say no.'

'I…' She sighed. 'I've done the mixing work and personal life thing before. It didn't work out.'

'Maybe because it was with the wrong person. Maybe Geoff wasn't the right one for you.'

'He wasn't,' she said definitely.

He paused. 'You said Julie wasn't the right person for me.'

'Yes.'

'And you're absolutely right. She isn't.'

'But…you're still in love with her.'

He shook his head. 'Not since a gnome barged her way into my life and started bossing me about.'

She narrowed her eyes. 'Gnome?'

'Come on, I had concussion. But I do remember,' he said, his voice low and husky, 'exactly what you looked like the morning after the storm. You have the most beautiful back, Mallory. Perfect skin. And your mouth drives me crazy. I remember how you feel, how you taste. And I want more.'

'We're in hospital!' she hissed, scandalised.

'And it's the wrong place to be saying this. I know. I don't care.' He brought her hand up to his mouth. 'I've already wasted too much time. I'm not going to waste any more. So ask me.'

'Ask you what?'

'If I want you to stay.'

'No.'

He smiled. 'Coward.'

'How you have the *hide* to say that, after—' she began.

He stopped her by bending over to kiss her on the mouth. Very lightly. But it was enough to stop her talking.

'OK. So you won't ask. I'll tell you anyway. I want you to stay, Mallory. For good. You make the room light up just by walking into it. A world without you would be a world without colour or depth or scent or meaning. And that's not what I want. I'm back in the real world now, and I want you with me all the way.' He kissed her fingertips again. 'So, did you mean what you told Eddie?'

'Eddie's all right?'

'Stop changing the subject. But, yes, Eddie's fine. They've warmed him up, his heart's absolutely fine—he didn't arrest on the way in to the hospital or anything— and you were right about the ankle and the Colles' fracture.

Cathy phoned here to tell me—she went straight to his bed-side.'

'What about Frank?'

'He and I had a little chat while you were asleep. I explained to him that Eddie needs Cathy most right now. And I told him there were other people who needed him.'

'He'll do the course?'

'He'll do the course,' Will confirmed. 'If I get the go-ahead from Paul.'

'If.' Odd how such a little word could be such a big thing.

'Oh, I think I will. I have the ultimate threat, you see—I'll set you on him when you're over your concussion. He wouldn't dare do anything other than agree. Small, scary and very determined. That's you.' His eyes met hers. 'Now put me out of my misery and tell me. Did you mean what you told Eddie? That you don't think I feel the same way about you as you feel about me?'

Mallory stared back at him. 'I don't know how you feel about me.'

'I love you,' he said simply. 'Yeah, there's the physical side of it.' And he actually blushed. 'I fancy the pants off you. And being this close to you and a bed is putting a lot of strain on my self-control. But you've got concussion and I've got fractures, so I'm going to be sensible.' His voice became husky. 'For a little while.'

The idea of what would happen when he stopped being sensible sent a shiver of desire through her.

'But it's not just that. It's *you*. I didn't think I'd ever fall in love again after Julie, but I can't stop thinking about you. I want to be with you. I want to spend the rest of my life with you. This is it. The real thing. And when you reach the summit of Everest, I'm going to be right there beside you.'

'Don't want to climb Everest.'

Will frowned, clearly not understanding. 'I thought that was your dream.'

'Was.' She smiled tiredly. 'I want to do medicine *and* climbing. Everest's too far away.'

'Where, then?'

'Here.'

He kissed the tips of her fingers. 'Well, I need a part-time GP. And I believe there's a certain MR team that would be interested in a permanent member.'

'Two permanent members,' she corrected. 'Hang on, are you offering me a job?'

'Not just at the surgery. What I've got in mind has…a few more hours. Like twenty-four seven.'

'Uh-huh.' Hopefully he was going to explain that. Because she definitely couldn't decipher what he meant. This concussion business would be seriously annoying if she could actually remember how to be annoyed.

He smiled wryly. 'This is the bit where I'm supposed to be down on one knee. I can't manage that yet—but I can't wait until I can. Did you know it's Valentine's Day today?'

Yes. And she'd even thought about buying him a card. Then had thought better of it.

'Will you marry me, Mallory?'

'Marry you.'

'Yes or no?'

'I'm dreaming. Hallucinating.'

'I'm real. And I can prove it.' He leaned over her bed and kissed her. This time he did it thoroughly.

'Mmm. I'm dizzy.'

His face went tight with concern. 'I'll call a nurse.'

She tightened her fingers round his. 'Not that sort of dizzy. *Dizzy* dizzy.'

His eyes glittered as he realised what she meant. 'We're going to have to work on those communication skills, Dr Ryman.'

'Promise?'

'Uh-huh. Talking of which, you still haven't answered me. Will you marry me?'

'I don't do domesticated,' she warned.

'Who cares? We have Mrs Hammond. And I happen to like cooking.'

'Sounds good.'

There was a long, long pause and finally he met her gaze. 'Um, do I get my answer, then? Yes or no?'

'Yes.'

'Yes, I get my answer or, yes, you'll marry me?'

'Yes, I'll marry you.'

And Will's whoop of delight was answered by a round of applause from the rest of the patients in the ward.

When Mallory was asleep again, Will tiptoed out to make a phone call. 'Hi, Mum.'

'She said yes,' Anne informed him. 'Congratulations, darling. I'm so pleased for you both.'

He smiled ruefully. He should have guessed that she'd already know. News travelled fast around here. 'I take my hat off to you and the spy network.'

'I know you're back on the MR team, too. Welcome back to the world, Will,' she told him. 'It's been a long time coming.'

'But worth it. Because I've found my Dr Right,' he said softly.

Four weeks later Will was sitting in the front pew on the right-hand side of St Peter's church in Darrowthwaite, his crutches propped beside him. Crutches which had been decorated with ribbons and tiny silver hearts, because he'd refused flatly to wait until he could walk on his own two feet before marrying Mallory. Renee, as the matron of honour, had said that if the crutches were going to be in the wedding photographs, they could at least *look* bridal. Mallory had simply laughed and said that Americans knew how to do parties properly and let Renee have her way.

As the first notes of the Wedding March filled the church, Will heaved himself to his feet and manoeuvred himself over to the aisle. Then he turned to watch Mallory walk down the aisle towards him on her father's arm.

She'd chosen a raw silk ivory sheath dress, saying that he was less likely to trip over it on his crutches. Her veil, edged with tiny seed pearls, fell from a silver and pearl tiara. She was carrying a simple sheaf of Calla lilies. Little Kelly Beswick—Mallory had insisted on her being a bridesmaid, as the person who'd brought them together in the first place—was tottering behind her down the aisle, wearing an ivory silk fairy dress and clutching a fairy wand in one hand and Renee's hand in the other. Renee, wearing a gold raw silk dress that matched Mallory's, was smiling broadly—a smile that was matched by every other person in the church, which had reached the point of standing room only.

And as for Mallory herself...Will had never seen anyone look more beautiful.

'Dearly beloved,' the vicar began, and Will stretched out his now cast-free left hand to take his bride's.

It didn't matter that he couldn't kneel during the service—because he could at least put both arms round his bride and kiss her thoroughly at the vicar's invitation. It didn't matter that he needed his crutches to walk down the aisle after they'd signed the register—nobody noticed when they had the whole mountain rescue team making a guard of honour outside the church with their ice axes for the bridal couple to walk through, liberally sprinkled with confetti. And it didn't even matter that he couldn't do the traditional first dance with his bride.

'Because we're going to have one hell of a party on our

first wedding anniversary, Will Cooper,' she told him. 'I'll claim my bridal dance then. And then we'll have a second honeymoon.'

'Party, yes. Second honeymoon...' He shook his head. 'I don't think so.'

'Why not?'

'Because,' he said simply, 'I'm not intending to let the first one end.'

Mallory leaned forward. 'Sounds good to me,' she said. And kissed him to seal the bargain.

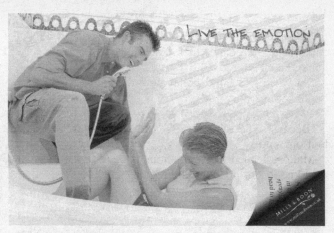

Modern Romance™
...seduction and
passion guaranteed

Tender Romance™
...love affairs that
last a lifetime

Medical Romance™
...medical drama
on the pulse

Historical Romance™
...rich, vivid and
passionate

Sensual Romance™
...sassy, sexy and
seductive

Blaze Romance™
...the temperature's
rising

27 new titles every month.

Live the emotion

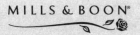

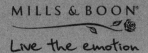

MILLS & BOON®

Live the emotion

Medical Romance™

OUTBACK ENCOUNTER *by Meredith Webber*

As a research scientist, Dr Caitlin O'Shea's usual problem is not being taken seriously – her stunning blonde looks get in the way! But she's not expecting her work in tiny Outback town Turalla to have so many other challenges – like Connor Clarke, the town's overworked doctor...

THE NURSE'S RESCUE *by Alison Roberts*

Paramedic Joe Barrington was determined not to give in to his attraction for nurse Jessica McPhail – he just couldn't get involved with a mother, and Jessica had to put her child Ricky first. But when Joe risked his life to rescue Ricky, he and Jessica realised that the bond between them was growing stronger by the day.

A VERY SINGLE MIDWIFE *by Fiona McArthur*

Beautiful midwife Bella Wilson has recently regained her independence – and she doesn't want obstetrician Scott Rainford confusing things. Twelve years ago their relationship ended painfully, and she won't let him hurt her all over again. But now, working side by side, they find their feelings for each other are as strong as ever...

On sale 6th February 2004

Available at most branches of WHSmith, Tesco, Martins, Borders, Eason, Sainsbury's and all good paperback bookshops.

0104/03a

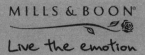

4 FREE

books and a surprise gift!

We would like to take this opportunity to thank you for reading this Mills & Boon® book by offering you the chance to take FOUR more specially selected titles from the Medical Romance™ series absolutely FREE! We're also making this offer to introduce you to the benefits of the Reader Service™—

- ★ FREE home delivery
- ★ FREE gifts and competitions
- ★ FREE monthly Newsletter
- ★ Exclusive Reader Service offers
- ★ Books available before they're in the shops

Accepting these FREE books and gift places you under no obligation to buy, you may cancel at any time, even after receiving your free shipment. Simply complete your details below and return the entire page to the address below. *You don't even need a stamp!*

YES! Please send me 4 free Medical Romance books and a surprise gift. I understand that unless you hear from me, I will receive 6 superb new titles every month for just £2.60 each, postage and packing free. I am under no obligation to purchase any books and may cancel my subscription at any time. The free books and gift will be mine to keep in any case.

M4ZED

Ms/Mrs/Miss/Mr ....Initials................................
BLOCK CAPITALS PLEASE

Surname ....

Address ....

....

....Postcode...............................

Send this whole page to:
UK: FREEPOST CN81, Croydon, CR9 3WZ
EIRE: PO Box 4546, Kilcock, County Kildare (stamp required)

Offer valid in UK and Eire only and not available to current Reader Service subscribers to this series. We reserve the right to refuse an application and applicants must be aged 18 years or over. Only one application per household. Terms and prices subject to change without notice. Offer expires 30th April 2004. As a result of this application, you may receive offers from Harlequin Mills & Boon and other carefully selected companies. If you would prefer not to share in this opportunity please write to The Data Manager at the address above.

Mills & Boon® is a registered trademark owned by Harlequin Mills & Boon Limited.
Medical Romance™ is being used as a trademark.
The Reader Service™ is being used as a trademark.